MW01139936

A

Charming Wish

Magical Cures Mystery Series

Book Three

Also by Tonya Kappes

Women's Fiction
Carpe Bead 'em

Anthologies
Something Spooky This Way Comes
Believe Christmas Anthology

Olivia Davis Paranormal Mystery Series
Splitsville.com
Color Me A Crime

Magical Cures Mystery Series
A Charming Crime
A Charming Cure
A Charming Potion
A Charming Wish

Grandberry Falls Series
The Ladybug Jinx
Happy New Life

A Superstitious Christmas

Never Tell Your Dreams

A Divorced Diva Beading Mystery Series

A Bead of Doubt Short Story

Strung Out To Die

Small Town Romance Short Story Series

A New Tradition

The Dare Me Date

Non-Fiction

The Tricked-Out Toolbox~Promotional and Marketing Tools Every Writer Needs

This book is a work of fiction. Names, characters, places, and incidents are the product of the author's imagination or are used fictitiously. Any resemblance to actual events, locales, or persons, living or dead, is entirely coincidental. All rights reserved. No part of this publication can be reproduced or transmitted in any form or by any means, electronic or mechanical, without the permission in writing from the author or publisher.

Edition: March 2013

Copyright © 2013 by Tonya Kappes

All rights reserved

License Notes

This ebook is licensed for your personal enjoyment only. This ebook may not be re-sold or given away to other people. If you would like to share this book with another person, please purchase an additional copy for each recipient. If you're reading this book and did not purchase it, or it was not purchased for your use only, then please return to the publisher and purchase your own copy. Thank you for respecting the hard work of this author.

Acknowledgments

Thank you really doesn't cut it when I think about the village it takes to publish a book. Tobi Helton has been a big supporter of my novels and came up with the perfect title for this third novel, A CHARMING WISH. Kellie Mounce is an amazing reader who won "name the genie contest," and Belur is a GREAT name! Mary Godschalk and Melissa Street are not only amazing beta readers, but I'm super proud to call them my friends.

Hugs and love to my guys (Eddy, Jack, Brady, and Austin). You guys are so understanding when it comes to deadlines and limited mom time. Especially since we moved during this novel. My life is nothing without you guys!

Chapter One

"Hear ye, hear ye," Faith Mortimer's voice echoed throughout the valley, down Main Street and straight into A Charming Cure as she announced the day's headlines from the *Whispering Falls Gazette*. "Be on the lookout for a storm brewing. Have you ever noticed the dark purple skies during storms? This message is brought to you by Wicked Good Bakery. Be sure to stop in and get your Peppermint Scone. Be sure to stop in Glorybee. Petunia Shrubwood has reported to our very own Police Chief, Oscar Park, that there has been a huge increase of stray animals. They are not animals from souls; they are the real live furry creatures. Be sure to keep healthy by taking your daily vitamin potions from A Charming Cure. Tell June you heard about this ad and get ten percent off. Whispering Falls Gazette is running a special. Get four weeks free with a six month paid subscription. See Faith Mortimer for details."

Immediately, I grabbed The Magical Cures Book and tuned out the rest of the morning paper headlines. I had a few minutes before I had to open my homeopathic cure shop, A Charming Cure, to make a quick protection potion. By the sound of Faith's report, something big was about to happen and I definitely wanted to be prepared.

Not that I thought I needed protection, but you can never be too careful. Faith could've been talking about anyone.

Following my finger down the index in the front of my book, I honed in on my intuition to see which protection spell spoke to me. Like always, the print on the right potion became bold, standing out from the rest.

"Ah, ha!" I quickly turned to the spell. "A level twenty-eight spell."

Level twenty-eight was a stage I had just started to work within and wasn't having a whole lot of luck in doing so. But I hadn't given up yet. As we say in the spiritualist world, "practice makes perfect."

I read the ingredients. *Four cups of spring water, one tablespoon of powdered iron, one teaspoon of Vervain, two tablespoons of sea salt, two tablespoons each of frankincense & myrrh, and a pinch of ground ostrich feather from a live ostrich.*

The feather might prove to be a bit challenging. Walking behind the counter, I ran my finger along the shelf of ingredients to see if I happened to have any ostrich feathers in stock.

"Of course not," I sighed, but eyed the sleeping white cat nestled on my stool, "Mr. Prince Charming," I sang. His fur would have to substitute. I plucked a tuft from his tail.

Meow! Mr. Prince Charming darted under one of the round display tables. The tip of his white tail was the only part of him that could be seen beneath the long red draped tablecloth. His tail slowly dragged on the floor.

"Chicken!" I blew a puff of air toward my bangs to get them out of my eyes. "Besides, you are my Fairy god-cat, not a scaredy cat."

I stood back and threw a pinch of Vervain into the bubbling cauldron. Shielding my face with my hands, I snuck a peek through the slits of my fingers. My potions had a habit of blowing things up.

The emerald toned tonic frothed, turning an onyx color and letting off a black pepper smell, circling around my fingers and up my nose.

"So far so good!" *Cough, cough.* I fanned my hands in front of my face. My charm bracelet jingled and jangled in the air. "A little smoky, sure, but nothing *tragic.*"

Mr. Prince Charming yanked his tail completely under the table, making me a little uneasy. I looked down and grasped my turtle charm, then gently touched the Celtic knot, dog charm, and the small owl. If something was about to happen, Mr. Prince Charming would've dropped a charm at my feet or on the counter to keep me out of harm's way. I was just being paranoid after all of those other…incidents.

Mr. Prince Charming had shown up on my tenth birthday with the turtle charm on his collar, and it wasn't until a little over a year ago that I was told he had been my Fairy god-cat all this time.

Fairy god-cat…hrrumph! I glared at the table. More like a scaredy cat.

Most little girls dreamed of having a Fairy Godmother like Cinderella. Well let me tell you, that was not how it happened in real life. I got a *cat.*

I let go of my bracelet, pushed a strand of my black bobbed hair behind my ear and rolled up my sleeves to finish this potion. Grabbing a handful of salt, I threw it in with a chaser of natural spring water and Mr. Prince Charming's hair.

Vroom!

A puff of smoke shot up and hung over the boiling pot. It fizzed and popped, and slowly I stirred the frothy draught until the bubbles turned into a slow boil.

I closed my eyes, and took a deep breath as I tried to tap into my intuition for any insight of upcoming danger.

Luckily, I have always had a wonderful sense of intuition, but going to Hidden Hall A Spiritualist University for intuition school was one of the best things I had ever done as a spiritualist. Not only did it help me tap deeper into my gift, but it also allowed me to understand my place in the spiritualist world.

When I was a baby, my parents lived in Whispering Falls until my spiritualist dad was murdered. The community moved Darla, my mom who didn't like to be called Mom, and me to Locust Grove, a nearby "normal" town.

Darla owned A Dose of Darla, which was a booth in the local flea market, and I had grudgingly worked there. What teenage girl wants to be seen at a flea market, much less be running a booth there? Surprisingly she did very well, but passed away right after I graduated from high school, leaving me in charge of A Dose of Darla.

I have to say that I think I did a fabulous job. The more homeopathic cures I made, or you could say potions, the more they sold. Customers started to flock to the booth. When the Whispering Falls Village Council discovered I had inherited my father's spiritualist gift, they came knocking. Only I didn't know anything about my gift until I visited Whispering Falls and realized it was the perfect town for my ornery cat and me.

Cough, cough.

"Level twenty-eight sure is smoky." I reached over and grabbed the Frankincense. My intuition told me to use just a dash.

The smoke cleared and the cauldron stopped bubbling, letting me know the potion making process was finished.

"That wasn't so bad," I called in Mr. Prince Charming's direction. The edge of the tablecloth looked like a beating drum. He batted at the loose hem. Directing my attention back to the potion, I knew I had to pick the perfect bottle.

I scanned the shelf on the wall that was full of empty bottles that just seemed to reveal themselves to me. Usually the right bottle would step up to the plate and glow after the perfect matching potion was made.

"Come on." I encouraged each bottle not to be shy as I took my finger and went down the line gingerly tapping each one. Nothing. Not a single bottle had a hint of a glow.

Glancing back over them, I couldn't help but wonder if level twenty-eight required some other sort of intuition skill that I hadn't quite mastered.

The Magical Cures Potion book, the only thing that Darla left me, flipped shut when I glanced in its direction.

Hmm...I started to walk over to take a look at it, but a bottle suddenly glowed like the sun. "It's about time," I said crossly, taking the bottle down from the shelf.

"I wondered what you were going to be used for." I eyed the twelve-inch hourglass shaped bottle that seemed too large for a potion. You can never have too much protection. . .at least that's what I thought.

The purple base glowed, showing off the gold specks throughout the glass, and ending in the tip of the glass cork. It was the most beautiful bottle.

"You?" I tapped the bottle and smiled. I had been waiting for the supplier of my smudging ceremonial grass, a Native American who blew in with the wind and out with the breeze, to come in before I used this particular bottle. It had dropped out of the last batch of sage he had brought in. I wasn't sure if he wanted me to have it or if it was in the bundle by mistake. But it sure was pretty. "Alrighty then."

Carefully I picked it up and gently placed it on the counter next to the cauldron.

"I do wish I knew how to get a hold of your owner." I eyed the bottle once more before I gently stirred the potion. The Native American didn't leave a way to reach him. He always said he knew when I needed a new supply and he was always on time.

I looked back over my shoulder, glancing at the smudging ceremony bundles. There was only one bundle left, which meant he'd be here soon.

With the ladle full of level twenty-eight protection potion, I dripped a little around the perimeter of the shop. What was left would go in the bottle and be put on a shelf for sale. It would sell in no time.

"Thrice around, circle bound. Evil sink into the ground," I chanted as each drop hit the floor.

The scent of chocolate chip cookies wafted around the room. That was the thing with potions. When I made a potion tailored to a customer, the potion took on the customer's most favorite scent. But that was *before* level twenty-eight. I made a mental note to figure out why this protection potion smelled of chocolate chip cookies. Not that I minded, but it definitely wasn't *my* favorite smell.

Which reminded me of my delightful stash of Ding Dongs behind the counter. With the last drip dropped, and before I put the leftover potion in the bottle, I took the foiled treat and carefully unwrapped it and took a bite.

Mmm, mmm.

Mr. Prince Charming darted out from under the table and jumped up on the counter. He was the first in line for a pinch. Lucky for him, he wasn't like every other cat who can't have chocolate. Fairy god anythings can eat just about everything, and he loved Ding Dongs just as much as I did.

I checked my watch. "I've got to get back to work." It was almost time to open and I wanted to make sure to get the lovely protection potion on the shelf.

Slowly I unscrewed the pointy tip and pulled, and then pulled harder.

"This must be really old." I tilted it to the side to show Mr. Prince Charming.

Hiss, hiss. His claws hit the glass bottle, shooting him off the counter and to the ground. Landing on his feet, he scurried across the room and scratched at the front door.

"What is your problem today?" I yanked the cork off and the bottle glowed red, burning my hand. "Ouch!"

I dropped the bottle, watching it bounce like one of those kid bouncy balls all around the room.

RROWR! Mr. Prince Charming ran back under one of the tables as the bottle bounced to and fro, landing on its side in the middle of the floor. Indigo smoke spewed up and swirled around, dancing to the sound of a kazoo.

Damn level twenty-eight. I really should have read the Magical Cures Potion book all the way through before I tried my hand at it. "Damn, damn, damn!"

Something told me there was more to level twenty-eight than what was in the potion book, but I was sticking to what I knew.

I reached down to pick the bottle up off the floor. It rolled to the left, and then to the right, making it difficult for me to grab.

Hiss, hiss. Mr. Prince Charming was nowhere to be seen, but he was letting his presence known.

Dropping to my knees, I reached over and pulled up the tablecloth.

"Finally!" the voice boomed out from behind me.

"Ouch!" I rubbed my head after I jumped up and hit it on the table. Potion bottles tumbled down and crashed on the floor.

"Oops," the same voice said, only a little more meekly this time. "I guess I should have said what I'm supposed to say."

My mouth dropped open.

"Yep. Your wish is my command." The large purple man stood before me with his hands on his hips. Rotating his body side to side, his bones cracked with every turn. He took his hands and placed one on each side of his face, twisting his head until it made a popping noise. "It gets a little cramped in there, especially after five-hundred years."

"You did it this time," Madame Torres, my snarky crystal ball, chirped from on top of the counter. "This isn't good. I'm going to have to agree with Mr. Prince Charming on this one."

"Well, you could've warned me," I hollered out, not taking my eyes off the man. Not because he scared me, but because I'd never seen a seven-foot tall purple-tinted man with a belly protruding over a yellow banana hammock and a pair of gold shoes sporting a jingle bell on each pointy tip. "What?" He glanced down his body to see what I was staring at. He patted his belly. "Yeah, I'm a little out of shape after five-hundred years."

"I. . ." I stumbled when I remember how the Gazette said something about a purple...hhmm...I tapped the palm of my hand on my head trying to remember exactly what the purple comment was.

Purple? Nah, it had to be a coincidence, even though he had created a little storm in my shop. But that was going to stop right now.

Hiss, hiss, Mr. Prince Charming wasn't amused with Whispering Falls newspaper headlines or the man.

"You have to unsubscribe from the newspaper and get that…that…whatever *that* is back in his bottle!" Madame Torres turned a flaming red, glowing throughout the entire shop. Her purple eyes appeared, taking up all the space in the ball. "Half of Faith's newspaper stories don't even come true! She's just too young to be a spiritualist. She needs to go back to Hidden Hall and work on her clairaudience skills."

Madame Torres rambled on and on about poor Faith Mortimer's spiritual gift. Granted, she should be able to hear anything inaudible from spirits, wind, or angels when they are predicting the future. There was one small, well, big problem. She only got half of it right. "And he is nothing but trouble I tell you!"

"Argh!" I was at a loss for words. The man hovered in the air with his arms crossed. I held up a finger. "Wait right there."

There had to be something in the Magical Cure Potion book…something, anything.

"I knew I should've taken those potion classes with all the levels." This had level twenty-eight written all over it.

"I'm waiting to hear what you want." Sarcasm dripped from his voice. "Honestly, I don't think you know what you want."

My mouth popped open, and my brows drew together. "Great, that's all I need...another smart-alecky spiritualist to deal with. Trust me, as soon as I figure out how to get you permanently out of that bottle so I can put my protective potion in, the better off we all will be."

"Amen." Madame Torres clapped and did spirit fingers. "And good luck with that task."

"What do you mean?" It was the first bit of advice she had offered up. "Madame Torres?" I questioned the coal-black crystal ball and tapped on the glass. She had gone into hiding. "Fine, be that way."

Before I could make it around the cauldron and look at my potion book, the front door of the shop flew open blowing in a gust of wind and Mr. Prince Charming ran out. The purple man disappeared into thin air and his bottle magically landed right back on the shelf where I found it.

The bell that hangs over the front door dinged as the Karima sisters bolted in.

"Did you hear the newspaper headlines?" Constance Karima waddled over to the broken bottles with her sister, Patience, closely behind her. "See," she pointed to the bottles and eyed Patience, "looks like the storm has already started in here."

"Now, now." I grabbed the broom and dustpan. I had to defuse the situation before it got any messier. Making sure mister purple man was staying put on the shelf, I kept one eye on him while I swept up the mess he had created. "Mr. Prince Charming did it when he was playing with the hem of the tablecloth." I pointed out the unraveled red thread. "You saw him dart out the door as soon as you opened it."

"Yep." Patience wrung her hands together. She curled her nose, causing her beady black eyes to squint. With her nose in the air, she took big long sniffs. She repeated, "Already started."

Chapter Two

The headlines in today's paper were a little strange and making a little morning visit to Faith Mortimer seemed to be in my future.

Faith was young, fresh out of college and starting to learn how powerful being a fortune teller could be.

"Are you going to find out what she's talking about?" Constance twiddled her little plump fingers. "And can you ask if there is going to be any deaths in the future?"

"Yes, deaths." Patience repeated, but didn't take her bulging eyes off the potion bottle on the counter. The purple man's bottle faintly glowed. She took a step toward it. Quickly, I untied my apron and casually tossed it on the counter, covering most of his glimmer.

"No. I'm not asking about any deaths." I brushed my hands off, and then crossed my arms.

"Single handedly, you are killing our business, June Heal." Constance's housedress swooshed as she shifted to the right, planting her hands on her hips. Her dress hiked up on one side revealing a tattered pair of black pointy-heeled shoes that were warn around the toes, making them a little more round than pointy. "And I mean that literally."

Patience's nose curled, causing her lips to furl. Intently she stared at me, making me a bit uncomfortable. They owned Two Sisters and a Funeral Home and handled all the services for all of Whispering Falls and most of the surrounding cities.

I've been told that the sisters had a way of making a service feel a little more like a celebration of life instead of the smell of death. Everyone walked away from A Two Sisters and a Funeral services, saying they felt their loved one was there and it was a little…well…*magical*.

I hadn't figured out their entire business, but my gut told me that I was about to learn more than I wanted to know.

"I'm sorry you feel that way, but I haven't saved any soul that was meant to go to the great beyond." I walked around, taking a few bottles from here and there, replacing the ones that had taken a tumble from the little storm that happened during the mister purple guy entrance.

"You give them all sorts of witchy medicine to prolong a broken heart, gout, or even protection." Her eyes drew together, casting a shadow on the balls of her cheeks.

"Mm, hmm. Protection." Patience's eyes darted toward the front window of the store. Petunia was flailing her hands above her head as she ran down the street. Her empty dog leash that was usually attached to her wrist was replaced with a long rope that reminded me of a cowboy's lariat.

We hurried over to get a better look. I opened the shades fully and we glued our noses to the glass.

"Is that a…" Patience Karima pushed her glasses on top of her nose.

"An ostrich," I gasped, unable to take my eyes off the plush feathers. "I need one of those feathers."

"What?" Patience snarled.

"Come on!" I tugged on Patience's arm to get her to follow me.

"I'm not going out there." Constance declared. "I need protection!"

We all stood there in awe.

The ostrich was getting the best of Petunia as they darted around and around in a circle.

"What are you doing, sister?" Constance toe-tapped her shoe and crossed her arms.

Patience was jabbing to the right and then to the left, looking as if she and the ostrich were in some sort of battle.

A bird and several small sticks flew out of Petunia's messy up-do as she tackled the feathery beady-eyed bird to the ground and threw her legs over the body of the creature. The ostrich jumped up and darted around as Petunia rode it like a horse, guiding it back to Glorybee.

"I guess that is one of the animals Faith was talking about." I referred to Faith's little newspaper report. "Ostrich," I sighed, making a mental note to stop by Glorybee. I did need some cat supplies, and maybe I could score a couple of ostrich feathers while I was there.

I could easily redo that level twenty-eight potion.

"Yep. All coming true." Constance shook her finger in my face, and drew near. Her eyes looked deep into my soul. "I'm telling you, June Heal, you'd better get this village back on its feet or we are all in trouble."

"All in trouble," Patience echoed in a hushed whispered, never once taking her eyes off that ostrich.

Chapter Three

"Whew! That was close!" The purple guy stood right behind me when I turned around.

"Geez!" I put my hand on my heart. "You scared me!"

"You knew I was here."

"I told you he was trouble." Madame Torres appeared in the crystal ball. This time, her hair was tucked up under a bright yellow turban with a lime green jewel positioned in the middle. Her eyes were lined in black liner, with thick mascara heavily applied to her lashes, along with red-rosy rouge and lipstick.

"If you know there is trouble in my future, aren't you supposed to tell me?" I reminded her of her duties as my crystal ball.

"You need to send her back to get fixed." Mister purple guy whispered in my ear, only it wasn't much of a whisper.

"Oh shut up!" Madame Torres boomed.

"You shut up!" He yelled back. "You are mad because you are stuck in that little round glass while I can hop in and out of mine."

He floated in and out of his fancy bottle to prove a point, a trail of smoke following him.

Madame Torres huffed and her ball went black.

"Stop!" I yelled at him on one of his return trips to his bottle. "If I wanted to police children, I would have had some of my own."

"Ta-da!" He said, sticking his foot out, arms extended to the side, with a big smile on his face. "Now you have me. Your wish is my command."

"Listen closely," I warned him. "I'm not going to wish anything. I'm going to find out exactly where you came from and return you to your rightful owner. Where *did* you come from?"

"Belur here, and I am here to serve you, Master." He stayed in his "ta-da" position with his mouth wide open in the biggest grin I had ever seen. "You opened the lid, so now I owe you."

"I understand that." I took a deep breath. "Belur?"

Pride was on his face as he nodded up and down.

"Who had you before me?" I asked. This way I could give him back to his rightful owner and get on with my day.

Tsk, tsk. He wagged his finger in front of me. "That is top secret! I can't tell you that. I've been with diplomats from all over the world. If I revealed all my masters I'd be breaking the number one genie rule." He blew on his knuckles and then polished them off on his small green bedazzled vest. "The things I could tell you," he cackled. "Especially all the affairs and bad dealings I was into when my master was a Hollywood star."

"Great," I held the bottle up and faced the opening toward him, "a loose-lipped genie." I shoved the bottle toward him.

It sucked him back in, leaving a trail of purple smoke behind, just in time for the bell over the shop door to ding again, letting me know someone was there.

"Adeline, how are you?" I rushed over to one of my biggest customers; at least she has been over the past couple of months.

"I don't know, June." She leaned her small frame against the door, letting out a sigh. She wrapped a strand of her sandy blonde hair behind her ear. "For some reason, I woke up this morning and was feeling a little. . ."

"Off?" I eyed her.

She snapped her finger and pointed at me. "Yes, off." She smiled, letting those beautiful teeth gleam. "I knew you'd know what to do. I swear---you are way better than my doctor."

I watched her walk around the shop as she babbled on about how she didn't like to go to her doctor's office anymore because they didn't get her like I did. But, I wasn't so convinced I was 'getting' her.

"You really should go to your doctor." I encouraged her. "I'm not a doctor. I just know how to put herbs together."

Every shop owner in Whispering Falls has a psychic power with a magical twist. I just happen to be able to read what's wrong with someone. They might think they were having heartburn, when in reality they were sick from a broken heart. Of course, I gave them a remedy with a little extra umph in it from my handy dandy cauldron.

The entire village is magical.

To an outsider, Whispering Falls was just a tiny town with a population of five hundred, set in the foothills of a few mountains in Kentucky. Most people who visited our little village didn't know how special we really were, but they felt the magic while they were here, which was why they continued to come back for more. Adeline was no different.

The first time I met her, she thought she needed a little help in the love department, when in actuality she only needed a little self-confidence.

"You knew I was 'off'." She rolled her eyes, and then continued to check out the shelf with the potion bottle sitting on top. "They say it is all in my head. They make me feel like I'm crazy."

Her words floated around in the air, giving my instinct a run for its money. I couldn't get a grasp on what was off either. *Feeling a little crazy?*

Hmmm…I had to take that as a clue to her inward feeling, but what was really going on?

The more she talked, the more my stomach ached. I had always been able to read someone, good or bad.

I shook my head and swallowed. Belur must have put me all out of whack.

"And I want my remedy put in *that* bottle." Adeline rolled up on her toes, her eyes sparkling as she tapped Belur's genie bottle. "I've never seen anything like it. Well,

not in person. It kinda reminds me of that really old show. .
." She brought her finger to her chin and tapped it as if
trying to remember.

"I Dream of Jeannie?" I finished her sentence.

She snapped again, "Yep! See, I told you, you are
good."

Adeline was a great customer, but she wasn't the
brightest bulb in the room.

"Anyway, I love it! And that is the one I want." She
reached out to grasp it.

"Stop!" I shrieked. She quickly dropped her hand. "I
mean, I'm not sure you *need* anything."

There had never been a time I hadn't given the
customer exactly what they wanted. Granted, bottles
glowed when they got the right potion mix, and on
occasion, I did let the customer pick. Since Adeline had
been a great customer, she was used to coming in and
picking out a bottle.

"But it speaks to me, just like you say, 'pick a bottle
that speaks to you.'" She reminded me of what I tell every
single customer who walks through the door of A
Charming Cure. "Plus you said I was 'off'."

I took her by the shoulders and steered her away from the counter.

"I did say that, but you don't need a potion today." I smiled and shook my head, my bob swinging back and forth. "You need to do yoga."

"Yoga?" Adeline's eyes popped open. "Really?"

"Yes." I dropped my hands from her shoulders and put them in the Namaste pose. "Sometimes we have to bring our core and body back in alignment. You are 'off', just 'off'.'"

I didn't know how I did it, but she fell for it, hook, line and sinker.

"Where can I do that?" I thought she was gone, but she stopped shy of the door. "Is there a yoga studio in Whispering Falls?"

"No, but I bet there is one in Locus Grove," I said. She had a good point. There had to be some spiritualist who did yoga. I wondered why no one had opened a shop here.

"Why don't you come with me?" There was a mysterious look in her eye as she looked between the bottle and me. She was making it awfully hard for me to read her.

"I don't have time." That was the truth. What little time I did have, I wanted to spend it with Oscar, the sheriff of Whispering Falls and my one true love. "Besides, who would watch the shop?"

She shrugged. "I don't know, but you have to have a life for yourself."

Little did she know, I did have a life outside of this shop...only it was with Oscar.

"I'll check it out and let you know." She rolled her shoulders forward and then backwards, following up with a few neck rolls. "Just thinking about yoga is making me feel better."

"I bet it is." My eyes squinted as I watched her walk out the door. I muttered, "Something is off with *me* today." I peered out the window to see if Mr. Prince Charming was around, but the only sight I saw was the Karima sisters standing across the street watching the shop, as if they were policing it or something.

"You need to march right over to the Mortimer's and find out what *that* headline is all about." Madame Torres' voice was low and demanding.

"Aww. . .give Faith a second chance." I continued to look out the window and down the street. My gut wasn't giving me anything. Nothing. Nada. Maybe I could use some yoga.

"They didn't give the witches of Salem a second chance when they were hung or burned at the stake." Madame Torres spat back. She wasn't going to let up until I found out just what was going on.

"We don't live in Salem. We live in Whispering Falls." Quickly I pulled at my charm bracelet on my wrist. I tapped the dangling silver baubles, hoping there wasn't a storm brewing. And if it was, at least I'd have my charms to keep me safe. "Is there something in my future I should know about? I'm feeling a little strange and I can't pinpoint it."

"Yeah, get old Alibaba out of here."

"I can hear you!" Belur shouted. The lid of his bottle shook from the vibration.

"My bad. Get Alkazam out of here." She tried again.

"Not my name! And you could use a trip to the Lancome counter at a mall." He wasn't going to let her have the last word.

"Big purple butthead!" The crystal ball looked like it was on fire, just like one of those projects in a glass blowing class.

"Really? Big purple butthead?" Belur cackled, sending Madame Torres in an all-out tizzy.

"You nogoodsonofa…" Madame Torres's words ran together. Her gritted teeth and bright red lips were the only visible part of her face in the globe. I grabbed her with one hand and my bag with the other, stuffing her deep within.

"I won't have this, you two." I didn't feel well and I wasn't their parent. I had to get over to the Mortimer's to figure out if there was something about to happen, and if Belur has anything to do with it.

Chapter Four

"Yoo-hoo! June!" Bella Van Lou owner of Bellatrix Baubles, Bella's Baubles for short, was walking down the sidewalk toward me, waving her hands in the air. The balls of her cheeks looked even more round than usual as her smile exposed the gap between her two front teeth. "I was just coming to see you." She dangled something from her fingertips. "Are you not opening the shop today?"

"I am. I'm just running down to Wicked Goods Bakery to make a quick visit with Faith." I used my old skeleton key to lock the ornamental gate in front of A Charming Cure.

Oh no. I wanted to look away when I realized she was holding a charm. A charm that had to be from Mr. Prince Charming.

"I have a little gift for you from Mr. Prince Charming." She flung her long blonde hair behind her shoulders and let it cascade down her five-foot two-inch frame. She held out the charm for me to take. "I have to say, he was adamant about this one. It's a little different from most of the charms he has given you."

Reluctantly, I took the purple stone encased in a silver mesh. Instantly, I knew it meant protection…strong protection. But, from what? Mr. Prince Charming definitely didn't like Belur and obviously, Madame Torres didn't either. It had to be something to do with him and I had to get in touch with the Native American who delivers all my grasses for the smudging ceremonies that I perform for the group.

"It's a rose quartz pendent that will need to be put on your bracelet." She reached out and touched my dangling charms from my wrist. "Immediately," she said sharply.

Immediately? That word caught my attention. I glanced up to find her eyes downcast.

"Have you been feeling alright?" Bella swayed back and forth, her eyes assessing me. "I mean, you look great. Are you letting your hair grow out a little?"

I was stupid. Bella's spiritual talent was astrology and she could read the stars and gems.

"I'm assuming I need protection from something?" I wasn't going to beat around the bush. "Any ideas as to what that is?"

"Now, June Heal," She took a step back and placed her hands on her hips, "you know that the number one rule in Whispering Falls is that you can't…"

"Yeah, I know." And I did know better. "You can't read another spiritualist. But Mr. Prince Charming can let you in on a little known secret that I can't know?"

"He is different." She reminded me. "He's a Fairy god-cat and he is keeping you safe. You just need to do as I say and let's get this on your bracelet."

Looking around Whispering Falls, the streets were starting to fill with up with customers who were milling around, going from shop to shop. There was no time for me to get her to put it on now; I planned to go see Faith.

I unclasped the bracelet and dropped it into her open palm.

"I'll be by after work to get it."

"Sounds good." She gestured for the pendent that I had tucked in the palm of my hand. "See you soon."

"Wait." I quickly pulled my hand to my chest. "Do you know the name of the Native American who supplies me with smudging grass?"

"Oh, Kenny." She smiled, exposing the gap between her teeth. "Such a soft spoken man, but he does bring me the best turquoise stones you have every laid your spiritual eyes on."

"Kenny?" I tried not to chuckle, but I did. He definitely didn't look like a 'Kenny'. He looked like he could be Pocahontas's brother.

"What?" Bella asked. She held her hand high above her head. "He's about yay tall with dark handsome features?"

"Yep, that's him." I nodded. "Do you know how to reach him?"

"No. He has a way of knowing exactly what we need and when we need it." Bella shrugged. "He blows in with the wind and…"

"Yeah, yeah, I know," I waved my hands around, and then held my palm out for her to take the pendent, "out with the breeze."

"What do you need him for?" She questioned.

"I need a few supplies." I lied. But there was no way I was going to tell anyone about Belur. He was a type of spiritualist that everyone wanted. If anyone found out he was in my shop they would beat down the door trying to get him. After all, who wouldn't want their wishes to be granted?

"He'll be back." She took the pendent and rushed back down the street toward Bella's Baubles. She hollered over her shoulder, "I'll bring it back later today."

I crossed the street, nodding and smiling as I passed the people on the street, keeping Wicked Good Bakery in my sights. The bakery was owned by Faith's sister and baker extraordinaire, Raven Mortimer. They shared the apartment over the bakery.

The aroma of fresh baked cookies floated through the air. I smiled, knowing Raven probably sent the inviting homemade goodie's smell throughout Whispering Falls. No one could ever resist one of Wicked Good's tasty treats, not even me.

I couldn't help but smile when I saw a little car parked in front of the shop with a big plastic cupcake on top and Wicked Good's logo plastered all over the sides.

"Good morning! I love the new car." I hollered to Raven. She was busy sticking all sorts of heavenly treats in a box for a waiting customer.

"Good morning. We have so many deliveries outside of Whispering Falls that I had to get something. Plus it's free promotion for the shop." She smiled, sending a sparkle from her white teeth to her onyx eyes. Her long black hair was piled high in a loose bun atop her head. "I'll be with you in a sec." She held a finger up.

Glancing around the charming confectionary, I couldn't help but think how far our relationship had come. Just a little over a year ago, Faith, Raven and I met while attending Hidden Hall A Spiritualist University. I had just found out that I was, in fact, a spiritualist and as every village has rules, Whispering Falls was no different.

They were classmates in my intuition class. Even though we got off on the wrong foot, in the end, we became friends, and that was when they moved to my magical little town.

Besides Raven's amazing pastry talents, her spiritual gift as an Aleuromancy was what had customers coming back. Messages and answers came to her in the form of her baking. The dough forms itself into shapes unbeknownst to her while little messages for incoming customers stick in the back of her head. Those customers always pick out the perfect pastry for them. Sometimes she could read like a medium, only the spirit wasn't standing there as most mediums say they are.

Faith was a Clairaudient spiritualist. She hears things beyond the naked ear. She can hear spirits, guides, and angels, or simply see into the future in some sort of mystical way.

Unfortunately, her passion was the written word. She was the editor of Hidden Hall's newspaper, but her spiritual gift wasn't cut out for that type of work. So when she decided she wanted to open the only talking spiritual paper known to any spiritualist community, we were a little skeptical.

And you could see why; most of the things she reported weren't very accurate, sending a lot of villagers into a panic.

"You be sure to go visit your grandmother." Raven handed the boxed up goodies to her customer. She must've known something was going on with the customer's grandmother from the bakery goods or she wouldn't have said that.

She crossed the black and white checkered floor, wiping her hands down her pink Wicked Good apron, embracing me with a big welcome.

"I've been thinking about you." She pushed me an arm's length away to get a look at me. She bit her lip, a sure sign she had something going on in the spiritual world for me to hear.

"You have?" I questioned, remembering the number one spiritual rule. "I'm guessing you aren't going to come out with it are you?"

"Can't. But if you ask…" she baited me.

"Actually I'm here to see Faith." I absolutely wanted to hear what she was chomping at the bit to tell me.

"First let me give you these." She swept back behind the counter, grabbing a box of what I knew was going to be a few freshly baked June's Gems, her version of my favorite Ding Dong treat. "And while I was baking them…"

"June, how are you? Are you getting your morning paper okay?" Faith emerged from the back of the bakery. Her onyx eyes twinkled with anticipation.

Their eyes were the only hereditary trait the two sisters had between them. Faith had long blonde hair to Raven's black, as well as being a Good-Sider Spiritualist while Raven was a Dark-Sider.

"*How rude*, sister." Raven scolded Faith just as the big sister always did. "I was telling her something before you interrupted."

"Geesh, I'm sorry," Faith said, but she didn't mean it. She continued, "Was it clear? The newspaper? I've been working on all the acoustics around these hills surrounding Whispering Falls."

"I can hear it loud and clear." I wrung my hands together. I didn't want to hurt her feelings. "That's the problem. You are very clear on what you are seeing or hearing,   putting people in a panic, not to mention getting the Karima sisters hopes up in getting a body for a funeral."

"I'm just reporting as I hear it, see it, feel it." She twitched her mouth back and forth. There was a little hurt look on her face. "That is what a good reporter with any reputable newspaper does."

"I know, but sometimes it's not right." I spoke with caution. "Remember the fireflies."

She leaned against the counter when I reminded her of the time the fireflies in the community, which were the souls of teenagers, were going to put on a spectacular Fourth of July light show with their glowing tails. It just so happened that there was also a paid advertisement about bug spray. She mixed the two up, and all the spiritualists, including me, ran out to buy a case of bug spray. Petunia was one big ball of mad when she reminded everyone that we couldn't do bug spray because of the teenagers.

The village was up in arms, and poor Izzy, the Village president, had to settle everyone down. It took days.

"One little incident." Faith held her long thin finger in the air. I glared at her. "Okay, four at the most."

"Do you think you could put the paper out a day later? You know, let the information that is coming to you simmer for a little bit? Give yourself some time to digest it and not just spit it out?"

That was one thing she should've learned at Hidden Hall…how to deliver the message in a suitable, not so stinging way.

"I agree with June." Raven pulled down one of the four oven doors. Grabbing a mitt, she pulled out a pan of blueberry scones.

"I don't know who you think you are, June Heal," Faith completely ignored what Raven was telling her and focusing her attention on me and anger shone on her face, "but if you think that some little herbalist is going to tell me how to run *my* business in Whispering Falls, you have another thing coming to you!"

"Maybe you can work on the delivery without scaring people. That's what gives our type of people a bad rap." Raven didn't waste time to take the mitts off her hands before she went over to comfort her sister. "But I have to say that June is spot-on this time."

Faith's onyx eyes bore into me. "You will regret trying to tell me how to be a clairaudient"

The beeping of a horn coming from the street caught our attention. The Karima sisters were slowly driving down Main Street in their hearse. Patience leaned out the window with a big ole smile on her face, causing the balls of her cheeks to make her eyes squinty.

"Got us one!" She shouted and pointed to the gurney in the back. The gurney had a white sheet draped over it with something that clearly looked like the outline of a body underneath.

Slowly I nodded to let her know that I saw it.

"Weird!" Faith commented and darted to the back of the shop. Her thunderous footsteps hit the steps as she went back up to the apartment, followed by a door slam.

"They are two sick old women." Raven leaned her head to the side to watch the spectacle drive off to the Two Sisters and a Funeral Home before turning back to me. "Anyway, Faith was right this time. Something is brewing and that's what I need to talk to you about."

Her hand shook as she lifted the box of June's Gems in my direction.

"I think I'd better sit down for this." I took the box and a seat at the café table nearest to the window.

Glancing down the road toward the funeral home, I took a June's Gem out of the box and stuffed it in my mouth as I watched the Karima sisters get out of the hearse and do a little dance around to the back before pulling out their client.

Chapter Five

Chills ran up and down my spine as Raven confirmed my intuition that something was gravely wrong. And I couldn't dismiss the fact that Faith had all but threatened me.

Faith stormed back down to the shop, flailing her arms as she rushed through the doorway.

"I admit I'm not spot-on, but there is definitely something not right in the air surrounding Whispering Falls. The spirits are chanting." Faith closed her eyes, swaying back and forth as if being soothed by some sounds. "It's a low murmur. Almost sad."

"Can you make out what the chant is about?" Most the time when we use chants in our spirit world, it's about something important. "Brewing good? Bad?"

There had to be some sort of information that she was getting that could translate into something useful. After all, I did receive a genie bottle that I didn't dare tell anyone about. Well, maybe Oscar, but no one else. Then there were the Karima sisters, hauling some dead body in here. The body obviously had to be from out of town, because if someone had died in Whispering Falls, the word would've spread like wildfire.

"Something about feathers." Her onyx eyes popped open, her mouth dropped into an O and then she slammed it shut. "But *you* don't have to believe me."

"What feathers?" I begged to know, thinking about the ostrich feathers.

"You. . .um . . .need to find something to replace your Ding Dongs." She fixed her eyes on me, there was hatred resting in them.

With my elbows planted on the table, I repeated, "Feathers, Ding Dongs?"

"Yes, something with feathers is surrounding you." Raven said in a hushed whisper as new customers began to file in. "Darla came in the form of the June's Gems. She said there was grave danger around your shop."

Darla was always coming up in my June's Gems. She never approved of Ding Dongs when I was little, which Oscar and I hid them from her, and she never would approve of my addiction to them now. Which reminded me, I had been running low on my stash and I needed to run off to Locus Grove to grab some from the local Piggly Wiggly.

"Speaking of feathers, do you know Kenny, the supplier of my smudging grass?"

"Yes, I know Kenny." Raven turned to see the new customers coming through the door. "He delivers my secret ingredient for your June's Gems. As a matter of fact, he's been late on his deliveries lately and I'm not happy with him."

She reminded me of the delicious box of treats I was holding in my hand. I sat down at one of the café tables waiting for her to finish up with the customers.

Sigh… the smell of delicious chocolate seeped through the creases of the box, making my stomach growl. With anticipation, I opened the box. If there was ever a time I needed a Ding Dong it would be now, and a June's Gem was the closest I was going to get until I drove into Locust Grove.

While Raven helped some of her customers, I chomped down on my treat and tried to figure out how I could channel Kenny to give Belur back to him. Belur had caused an awful stir with Madame Torres. She didn't want him around and I certainly didn't have time to babysit another spiritual guide in my life.

"What is that all about?" Raven interrupted my thoughts. "You are devouring that Gem and that means you are stressed."

I pulled on her apron so she had to bend down to my chair, and I whispered, "I think I have Kenny's genie."

I knew if I told Raven, I could trust her. I had to tell someone before I exploded.

"A real, live genie?" She sat down, looking out the window while rubbing her hands together. "I'd love a real, live genie."

"No you wouldn't." I stood up, shaking my head. "He's clumsy and would have flour all over this place. Besides, he really doesn't belong in Whispering Falls. He needs to go back. He's going to be gone by the end of the week if I have to drive him to wherever he belongs."

"If he isn't, I'll take him." She didn't blink.

I put my hand on the front door of the shop, and then turned around to find Faith and Raven staring at me. "Wait until I get my hands on Kenny for slipping that genie into my bundle like that!"

I stormed out of the shop and down the street. Isadora Solstice, owner of Mystic Lights, was how I first found out about Kenny when I moved to Whispering Falls, and he showed up at A Charming Cure for payment when I had no idea who he was.

She was the village council leader. Surely, she'd know how to get in touch with him.

Chapter Six

"I'll be right with you," Isadora, Izzy for short, chimed from the back of the shop.

It gave me an opportunity to look around at all the fancy light fixtures and designs she had recently stocked on the floor. There were many different styles. Anything you could imagine and beyond could be found in Mystic Lights, even crystal balls.

That was how I acquired Madame Torres, or rather she found me. A crystal ball picks their owner, not the other way around. Sort of like cats.

The first time I walked into Mystic Lights, Madame Torres lit up the shop like fireworks on the Fourth of July. It was the most spectacular light show I'd ever seen. At the time, I didn't realize I was part of this entire spiritual world, but everyone else in Whispering Falls knew.

Izzy came to my home in Locust Grove, looking for a homeopathic curist to open a shop in Whispering Falls, only I had no idea she was looking for me.

"June dear, I'm so happy to see you." She shuffled from the back. Her normally perfectly groomed A-line skirt was wrinkled and her pointy-toed shoes were more tarnished than usual. "I've been meaning to stop by and talk to you about the village council meeting tonight."

Tonight? Damn! I had forgotten.

"In light of the newspaper article, I'm afraid you are going to have to do a protection smudging ceremony." She tapped the pads of the fingers together. "And another little favor."

"Yes, we will get to that favor in a minute." I held my finger in the air to stop her. There was never a better time to ask about Kenny than now. She brought up the smudging ceremony and he was who I got most of the bundles from. "How can I get in touch with Kenny?"

Izzy pushed her long blonde wavy hair behind her ears and her naturally pink skin turned abnormally pale. She stepped forward, curling her arm around my waist. "Don't you worry about him. He blows in with the wind as you need things."

She walked me back to the door and opened it with her free hand.

"We will see you tonight at the ceremony." She winked and sent me on my way.

"Wait!" I put my hand in the air. "What was the other favor?"

"Oh," Izzy's mouth formed an O, and then she smiled. "We will discuss that a little later."

Before I could protest, the air was filled with Faith.

"Good afternoon," Faith's voice boomed through the air, making me pause. I pushed the door to Mystic Lights open as Izzy pushed back from inside the shop. I had more I needed to ask her. I had to get in touch with Kenny and she was my only hope. Faith continued, "I wanted to make a quick news bulletin that is sponsored by Mystic Lights. Be sure to stop in for a crystal ball tune-up or a new light fixture so you can perform your magical gifts in the bright light." She cleared her throat. "In light of the recent news, a smudging ceremony will be held at dusk at the Gathering Rock. There will be an impromptu village meeting following. All need to attend."

I pointed to the sky above me and continued to push with the other hand. "Did you hear that?" I questioned Izzy.

Her hair was flinging side to side as she bore down on the door handle to keep me out. "Hear what?"

"Let me back in." I grunted.

"June, I'm busy today."

"Did you hear the announcement about the smudging ceremony from the paper?" And by paper, I meant Faith.

"Oh, no. I don't subscribe." When I let my guard down, the door slammed in my face, I could hear the clink of the deadbolts locking one-by-one down the door, followed by the clacking of Izzy's shoes.

Yes, there was a storm brewing. And I'm not fully convinced it all had to do with Belur.

"Shouldn't you be working?" I turned around to find Petunia questioning me. She had a long stick with a wire hoop on the end of it. Her soft brown hair sat atop her head in a messy knot. A few feathers that stuck out reminded me of Kenny.

"I am." I bit my lip. "Sort of. Listen, I'm doing that smudging ceremony tonight and I was wondering if you knew how I can get in touch with Kenny, the guy who brings my bundles to me."

Just then, the big ostrich ran across the road and back toward Petunia's shop, Glorybee.

Petunia darted off, shouting behind her, "Damn thing! He continues to get loose and I'm going to have to pluck him! And no! I don't know how to get a hold of him. Ask Izzy!"

"I did." I ran behind her toward the Whispering Falls sheriff's department, holding my arms straight out just in case I got lucky and got a handful of feathers. "I need one of those feathers!"

We had the ostrich pinned between us and the sheriff's door was behind him.

"Do not look at his beady little eyes," Petunia's hands were out as she stood inches from the bird, ready to pounce. Slowly, she swayed back and forth as if she was about to launch, but I knew it was now or never.

I leapt toward the feisty bird, grabbing a whole lot of nothing and falling to the ground. The bird took off and Petunia jumped over me.

"What did you do that for?" She screamed, as she twirled the big stick over her head, trying to rope him like a bull-roper would rope a bull.

The ostrich and Petunia show was much more fun to watch as she swung her stick in the air, hoping to get the metal loop around the big bird's neck, but to no avail. The bird did a couple quick side-steps and Petunia lost him.

"What was that?" a voice asked behind me.

I jumped up as Patience Karima scared the living crap out of me. There was a deep-set curiosity in her eyes.

"It's one of those stray animals that the paper had reported. Somehow, we are getting an abundance of strange animals, including that ostrich." Off in the distance, we could see Petunia flailing the stick in the air as soon as she was close enough to wrestle the feathery creature. He was much quicker than she was.

Petunia darted to the left; the ostrich darted to the right. Petunia's messy up-do began to fall. A Blue jay flew right out of her hair, leaving a trail of twigs to follow.

Petunia plopped on the ground as if she had given up. The ostrich stopped, focusing his beady eyes on her as though they were playing a game. His feathers gleamed in the sunlight, dancing in the wind, teasing me as if someone was eating a Ding Dong in front of me and didn't offer me one.

"I see that you have a fresh soul to bury." I said to Patience as I pointed toward the hill at the end of Main Street where Two Sisters and a Funeral was located.

The spiritual world believed that if you kept your dead on the outskirts of the town, it would send their souls out into the world and not into the village to be stuck in the in-between. Petunia was all too familiar with the in-between souls, as they come back as animals. But not these strays. They were plan ole animals that apparently showed up overnight.

"Mmhmm." Patience was aloof. "Constance wants me to go to A Cleansing Spirit Spa to get some natural nail polish. He has a lot of tobacco stains that we can't seem to get clean. He was a tobacco farmer. So, best we can do is cover it up."

"He obviously isn't local."

"Naw." She shifted her plump hips to the right, leaning a little closer. "It's only a one person viewing. That's it. No funeral. Nothing. They didn't have a lot of money, but we are desperate. We jumped at it since you've been taking all the business."

"Now listen here," I shook my finger in front of her face. "I didn't do any such thing."

"Patience!" Constance called out from the front entrance of The Gathering Grove Tea Shoppe and tapped a finger on her nails. Her eyes lowered, giving me a glare to remember. "The polish!"

Patience didn't need to hear anymore. She scurried off without another word and Constance disappeared back inside The Gathering Grove.

"Why aren't you working?" Oscar Park sauntered out of the police station looking mighty handsome in his blue Whispering Falls sheriff uniform, his sorcery wand sticking out from the baton holster. His crystal blue eyes clung to mine. He had two cups of coffee, one in each hand. "I got you a coffee and stopped by to give it to you."

I took it along with a kiss.

"You aren't going to believe, the strangest thing happened," I took a sip, "but I can't talk about it now. Not only do I have to get ready for the smudging ceremony, I have to find out how I can get in touch with Kenny."

"Who's Kenny?" Oscar asked, showing a little bit of his jealous side. Which I didn't mind because it was kinda of cute on him.

"He's that Native American who delivers all of my bundles. You know," I waved my hand in the air, "the one who blows in with the wind and out with the breeze."

"Vaguely." He smiled. I looked away in a desperate attempt to resist the captivating grin. There was no time to play boyfriend, girlfriend. I had to get Belur out of Whispering Falls and fast. "I can see other things are on your mind. I will see you later tonight."

He nodded toward A Charming Cure. I glanced over. There was already a line six customers deep. Trying to find Belur's real owner was going to have to wait until after work…after the smudging ceremony.

Chapter Seven

A Charming Cure was busy. As soon as one customer left, another customer walked through the door. One after the other, they filed in, picking up the bottles, reading the labels and placing them back on the table.

They seemed to know what they wanted and my intuition didn't go off like an alarm, which told me that everyone was in tune with their souls and real needs. That made a good day for me.

Every once in a while, I'd glance out the shop's front windows to see if Mr. Prince Charming was anywhere around, but I didn't see a flitter of a white tail anywhere. He knew I would pester him about the new pendent charm, and I will.

With a little time between each customer, I had to make a potion for Faith. I had a lot of concern over her lack of accuracy in her spiritual readings from her gift of clairaudience. Since I encouraged the Mortimers to move to Whispering Falls, I felt somewhat responsible for them, especially Faith. I felt a little pressure to make sure she started getting her readings as accurate as possible.

Especially if she was going to have the whole community up in arms.

Before disappearing behind the partition on the far end of the counter, I took a quick glance around to see if any customers needed my help. Slowly I inhaled, letting my intuition take over. Nothing was out of whack, or so it seemed, which was odd with this many customers in the shop at once. Everything seemed well with the world, so I flicked the cauldron on and began to think of Faith.

Biting my lip, I closed my eyes before running my finger along the line of spices. I had to have a clear image of Faith in my mind before the right ingredients would jump out at me.

Mugwort. I smacked my hands together just as the herb flashed in my head. Many spiritualists used Mugwort to help promote their psychic powers, and it was exactly what I needed for Faith.

"And a little pinch of parrot dander, along with a pinch of salt," I said to myself as I plucked the items off the shelf and tossed them into the pot.

With each dash, the cauldron began to bubble. The glowing substance swirled counterclockwise until the sapphire colored mixture took on a cerulean tone.

With my hands twirling over the boiling fluid, I whispered, "Hear today, lead the way. Help Faith predict the truth today."

Instantly, the substance stopped and the cauldron turned off. A faint glow, like a candle, illuminated the bottle shelf. Quickly I went around the counter and took the hot pink stout bottle off the shelf.

"Excuse me." There was a gentle touch on my shoulder from a young man that stood about five-foot-six with thinning light brown hair.

"Yes, can I help you?" I held the bottle firmly in my hand. Like a lightning bolt, it hit me. "Actually, I'm thinking you are looking for…" I tapped my chin with my finger and started to make my way over to the potions on the wall. "This." I took the hair tonic brew and held it out to him.

He adjusted his glasses so he could read the label. He'd be a mighty fine looking young man if he only did a few things to help change his appearance. And from my intuition, that was exactly why he was there. The look in his eyes told me I was more than right.

Meow, meow. Mr. Prince Charming scurried through the door when it swung open. Bella marched in behind him with my charm bracelet dangling from her fingertips.

"I'll get this all together and let you know when it's ready." I smiled at the man, and gave a knowing glance Bella's way, but scowled at Mr. Prince Charming.

She leaned on the counter, arms crossed, with Mr. Prince Charming backing her up.

"I had to get this over to you fast." Her eyes darkened with each word that escaped her mouth.

Hiss, hiss. Mr. Prince Charming batted his right paw in the direction of Belur's bottle. I didn't even look that way, so Bella wouldn't take note. But she did anyway.

"Mm-hmm…" She gave a sideway glance, and then nodded to Mr. Prince Charming like she knew what he was thinking. "Just put it on." She grabbed my wrist and clasped the bracelet. She fiddled with it and held my hand in the air as the bracelet dangled. "Hmmm?"

I shook it. "Yea, something is off." I noticed it didn't sit at the base of my hand like it had before she put the pendant on it.

Without another word, she unclasped it, scuffled across the floor, and out the door. I set Faith's bottle down. It was more important than ever to get her to take the potion, even though it was against the village rules. But how was I going to get her to take it without her knowing?

Belur's bottle lit up. My eyes grew big. The last thing I needed was his big ole body dangling in mid-air with a shop full of customers.

"Hey, hey, hey," Madame Torres shouted from the crystal ball. "You better stay put!"

Instantly his bottle turned back to normal and so did my heartbeat.

Meooowl. Mr. Prince Charming rubbed up against the bundles of sweet grass for the smudging ceremony.

"You are a genius." I picked him up and snuggled him close.

I could use the smudging ceremony to get the potion in Faith. I would make a drink for everyone to stay safe, only her drink would have the potion.

Someone clearing their throat caught my attention.

The balding man stood at the counter.

"Oh, right." I grabbed his bottle off the counter and hid behind the partition. Not only did he need a little hair thickener, he needed a little severed fledgling finger to help correct his eyes. He would be looking dapper in no time.

"Here you go." Vigorously I shook the bottle to make sure it was going to start working as soon as he rubbed it into his elbows. "Be sure to rub it really good into each elbow every single night before bed."

He fumbled with the bottle and adjusted his glasses before holding it an inch away from his nose to re-read the label.

"Yep, right there in the directions. Rub on each elbow before bedtime." I nodded with a huge grin on my face. This was where the magic came in. Originally, the bottle said to use it like gel if the client only wanted to use it to help with thinning hair.

My intuition told me that he wanted to help with his overall appearance and automatically the new ingredients changed the label. Magic.

Chapter Eight

"Can we go home now?" Madame Torres was not eager to discuss anything that was going on. We were in over our heads and I had to figure out a way to get out of it. Her eyes darkened as she glanced over at Belur. "It's closing time and I have no desire to be in here *with him* any longer than I have to."

I was shocked to see that she was right. It *was* closing time.

"Have you had any other thoughts about big blue?" Madame Torres appeared as I used the Cauldron Clean-Up to make my pot shiny and new.

Mr. Prince Charming barely lifted his head off the stool. He was all curled up and comfortable.

"Have I?" When have I not? I tossed the feather duster around the tables and bottles to get any dust off from the day. "Of course, but I can't help but think the headlines had to do with him."

Walking into the back of the shop, I grabbed a few pre-made potions to restock the shelves, plus straightened a few as I went along. Thoughts swirled around in my head like a tornado.

"I really wish I could get in touch with Kenny." I hollered over my shoulder as I picked up the potion I had made for Faith, and then placed it in my bag. "For the life of me, I have all this spiritual power, but I have no clue how to reach him."

Looking around, I searched for a fancy bottle to put some tap water in. I had to be sure to encourage everyone to take a sip as a new part of the ritual, as well as slip in the Mugwort when it was Faith's turn.

With everything stocked and put away, I put Madame Torres in my bag. "Let's go." The bundle of sage and sweet grass was ready to be used. I glanced up at Belur's bottle, but it was dark.

Meow, meow. Mr. Prince Charming jumped down and sat at the door.

"He must be asleep." I nodded toward Belur, because I was sure if he were awake, he'd create some sort of havoc before we left, or insist he come with us, which was not going to happen, especially at a smudging ceremony. "I don't know anything about genies and don't want to know."

I flipped the light off and locked the doors behind me. Petunia was sweeping the floor when I looked into Glorybee's window on my way to the ceremony. The live tree in the back of the store was filled with green leaves and beautiful birds of all shapes and colors. The hedgehog and squirrel were taking turns batting a nut between the two of them as they sat under the tree.

There was no sign of the ostrich.

Tapping on the window, I waved at Petunia. Her hazel eyes had flickers of gold specs as she smiled and motioned for me to come in.

"You were busy today." She shuffled around the store with the broom.

"It was a good day." I grabbed the other broom that was leaning up against the counter and headed over to the cat aisle to help her out. "Did you find the ostrich?"

"The strangest thing." She put down the broom and started to fill the bird feeders that were all over the store. A flock of blue jays flew behind her as she dragged the stepladder along. "That darn ostrich is gone. Again."

"I don't know much about ostriches, but where in the world did that come from?" I picked up a loose feather off the ground. I inspected it as I twirled it around in the air. "Is this an ostrich feather?"

Petunia put the stepladder away and came over to look at the feather.

"Naw, that's the macaw's." As soon as she said it, the multi-colored bird flapped way up into the tree.

Ostrich, ostrich, bad bird, bad bird. Squawk!

"Don't mind him." Petunia scowled. "I have to learn to watch what I say around that darn bird. He's one of *them*."

"One of them?" I questioned, still twirling the feather. I had hoped it was one of the ostrich's. Not that it would have helped me with the Mugwort tonight, but it might come in handy another time.

She leaned in, and so did her up-do. She whispered, "One of the ones that just showed up." Her eyebrows lifted.

"Oh." I walked over to the tree to get a better look at the big bird. "Hey there."

Hey there, hey there. Bad ostrich. He flapped his wings in delight. *Come to momma, come to momma. Things lookin' up, lookin' up.*

"Poor guy." I tilted my head and he mocked me. "He must be missing his mom. I'm sure the rightful owners will step up soon."

I looked around for Petunia to answer me, but the door to the storage room was swinging.

"What did you say?" Petunia emerged with her infamous dog leash strapped on her wrist without a hint of a dog at the end of it.

"Good evening, June." Gerald Regiula walked into the shop. He took off his top hat and tipped it to the side.

"Hi, honey." Petunia locked one arm in Gerald's elbow. "It's a good night for a smudging ceremony. If you can throw in a little blurb about the owners of these animals, I'd be mighty appreciative."

"We'll see." I patted my bag where the Mugwort and Madame Torres were deep inside. "We will see."

I followed Gerald and Petunia out of Glorybee and up the hill toward the Gathering Rock.

She leaped forward as the leash tugged on her arm. "Stop that," she spat at the leash. "I told the teenagers to keep an eye out for any unusual activity tonight. I'm not at all happy with the newspaper headlines today."

Without saying a word, I too hoped that after Faith took a little sip of the 'protection water' the headlines would get much better.

The Gathering Rock was beyond the lake and right before the edge of the forest. It was where we held all of our ceremonies.

Eloise Sandlewood emerged from the woods with her incense swinging to the right and to the left. Smoke emitted from the tiny holes in the metal container on each downswing. Her emerald eyes stood out against the long red cloak and her short crimson hair.

"What's she doing here?" Gerald cleared his throat before we approached the circle of villagers that had already gathered.

Normally Eloise didn't come to the meetings. She was a Dark-Sider who was more than content to live in her tree house deep in the woods, taking care of her garden and doing morning cleansing rituals through the streets of Whispering Falls as the other spiritualists slept.

She was a Holistic Cleanser. She cleaned out the evils from villages as well as made many herbs that supplied A Charming Cure. In fact, Eloise and Darla were best friends until Darla moved me back to Locust Grove to have a "normal" upbringing.

With a knot in my stomach, I watched Isadora sweep across the crowd to greet Eloise. With a few hushed whispers between them, they glanced over at me. Turning to the Gathering Rock, I pretended to organize all the herbs and items I needed for the ceremony.

Trying not to notice them both coming toward me, I bent down and situated the emerald rock next to the match.

"June, can we speak with you?" Eloise asked with a motherly tone.

"Sure." I stood up, brushing my hands down my jeans to knock off any debris from crouching down on the ground.

There was a crowd gathered around the Karima sisters.

"Oh, he's a good one." Constance rolled up on her toes as the glee in her voice escalated. "And we are getting paid for a full funeral when there isn't even going to be one."

"Full pay," Patience nodded and repeated. "Mm-hmm…full pay."

I felt sorry for the poor guy who was dead, but it was nice not to have the Karima sisters on my hiney about ruining their lives.

"We have something we need to tell you." Isadora stood in front of Eloise. I glanced over her shoulder. Eloise's hands were clasped together up by her nose as if she were praying. "It's time, June."

"Yes, I'm ready. I have all the bundles ready to go." I pointed to the Gathering Rock where my pile of tools was laying.

"No, I mean it's time for me to step aside and let the younger generation take over." She planted her hands on my shoulders. "It's time for you to take your rightful position as the leader of the spiritual village."

"That is why I'm here with the incense." Eloise gestured to the long chains dangling from her wrists. "I grew the special herbs to help ease the transition."

"I will tell everyone about what is going on." The crowd was getting bigger. "Then we can continue with the ceremony."

"I'm not sure about this." There was a deep tug at my gut. It wasn't a good or bad tug, but a little nudge telling me that I had to proceed with caution.

"Are you kidding me?" Eloise's emerald green eyes were electrified. "Your parents would be so proud and thrilled for you. This is an honor that doesn't come along every day. Not in centuries in fact."

Isadora's wavy long blonde hair ebbed and flowed as she nodded her head while listening to Eloise explain the importance of the opportunity. It wasn't that I didn't understand what an honor it was. It was the fact that I had only been a spiritualist, a true spiritualist, for less than two years. There had to be more qualified villagers than me for the job.

Mr. Prince Charming darted around my ankles, doing his signature figure eights. Warmth, comfort, and a sense of security filled my soul.

"I'll do it!" I yelped. Instantly I wanted to take it back. There was an instant message from my intuition, but it was cloudy. I gulped, trying to catch my breath.

"Great!" Izzy clapped her hands. "Everyone gather around. I'm sure you are wondering why we are having an emergency village meeting and ceremony tonight."

"Are you okay?" Eloise touched my arm in a motherly way. "You look a little pale."

"I'm fine," I lied. I was far from fine, but I had already committed to this. Something was off now more than ever. "We need to start."

The three of us joined the circle of villagers. I pulled the water and chalice out of my bag, slipping the vile of Mugswart into my pocket.

Slowly, I poured the water in the large cup.

"Tonight we are going to do things a little different. Then Izzy is going to make an announcement." I held the chalice in the air. "Special, special drink tonight, protect us with all your might."

As I walked around, I handed each of them the chalice, making sure Faith was last.

"Oops." I looked into the chalice. "Looks like I need to refill."

I slipped the vile out of my pocket and poured it into the chalice before handing it to Faith. She didn't say a word, but her dagger stare was enough to let me know she hadn't forgiven me for what I had said to her at Wicked Good.

She took the cup, and like a good Good-Sider, she drank it all.

The wind whipped overhead causing the leaves to do a tunnel dance around the meadow. It was nothing like I had ever seen. It was as if the wind had some sort of choreographed dance.

"Did you see that?" I asked Eloise, pointing in the direction of the dance.

"What?" Eloise strained her eyes in the direction I had pointed.

Shaking my head, I started to walk back over to the Gathering Rock to light the smudging bundle. "Nothing," I said, fiddling with my wrist, I wished I had my charm bracelet.

If Eloise didn't see it, no one else saw it either. A sure sign that Faith was right...something was brewing.

The air was thick and silent as the villagers waited with anticipation for Izzy to speak. You could have cut the tension with a knife. Each pair of eyes told a story of worry. That was what had come from having a newspaper in Whispering Falls and a Clairaudient being in charge of it. They focused on Izzy's words. We all know that we can't change the outlook of our future.

"It's been a great pleasure being the leader of such a wonderful community of spiritualists." Izzy's cloak dragged behind her, leaving a trail of dust clouds as she walked around the circle. Gently, she reached out and touched every single person who had gathered. The crowd was so big that it was hard to hear what she was saying from the other side. "We have seen a lot of changes, going from being a community of Good-Siders to a community of all spiritualists, including the Dark-Siders." She grabbed Eloise's hand. The two friends smiled at one another. Their affection was apparent.

"It's all because of our very own June Heal, who was born into this community." She gestured toward me. I shuffled my foot in the grass, hoping they couldn't see my red face in the dark night that had fallen upon us. "It's time. Time to pass the torch to the younger generation. June Heal is going to be our new council leader who will take us into the future."

A round of applause and shouts sounded out into the night sky. The fireflies fluttered about, creating a flurry as they shot into the sky forming a thumbs-up.

"Are you kidding me?" Petunia Shrubwood shrilled as Gerald put an arm around her to console her.

She shrugged away so fast, Gerald's arm flung up into the air.

"Um…Petunia!" I yelled. "Just a few months ago you said I'd make a great Village President!" My mouth dropped open and slammed shut. I turned to Eloise. "I think she's mad."

Eloise curled an arm around my shoulder, as the entire community watched Petunia stomp down the hill toward town.

Out of the corner of my eye, I saw a flash. Looking in the direction of the woods, a big figure stood with his arms crossed. The shadow of the feather headdress lay on the grass as the moon created a spotlight.

Like a deer, Kenny gracefully leapt and jumped down the hill toward A Charming Cure.

"I've got to go!" I held a hand up, knowing I had to catch him to give him Belur. It was my only opportunity to give him back until the next time he blew into town. My little whisper in the wind must've summoned him and he came!

"No! Don't follow them!" Bella cried out, almost sounding in pain.

I did it anyway.

The fog was starting to roll in for the night. It was hard seeing in front of me as I ran after him. The only light was the small streetlights that dotted Main Street. The only sound was the stampeding of the crowd running after me.

"You can stop following me." I stopped walking and turned around to face the villagers. "I'll be back before the ceremony."

"But you are the village leader. We thought you were taking us somewhere." Constance Karima shouted from the group.

"You are supposed to dismiss us, like Izzy does." Chandra Shango held her perfectly manicured hands in the air, reminding me I needed to go to Chandra's shop, A Cleansing Spirit Spa, to get my nails done.

"Dismissed!" I threw my hands in the air. Not only did I have to figure out the level twenty-eight potion, now I had to learn and abide by all the rules of Whispering Falls. Little did they know that I was good, no, great at altering them to fit my own spiritual needs.

I was going to have to rethink this whole village leader thing.

"Help!" Someone screamed from the direction of A Charming Cure. "Murder!"

Murder?

I darted off in the direction of the blood-curdling scream with Mr. Prince Charming on my heels.

Hiss, hiss. He took off in front of me, leading the way with the crowd not too far behind.

"What is with all this fog?" I swept my hands in front of me. The fog parted. We saw Adeline standing at the steps of A Charming Cure along with Petunia and Gerald. A pair of feet were sticking out from the opened front door of the shop… Kenny's feet.

"Sister, it's our lucky day," Patience gasped, "it looks like we got us another one."

Chapter Nine

"Let's go over this one more time." Oscar stood over a distraught Petunia, who was sitting on the stool next to the counter. I wasn't sure if she was crying from finding Kenny in the doorway of my shop, or from the pain of the crow's claws that was perched on her shoulder. "You got upset at the smudging ceremony and ran down the hill to get away."

She nodded and a few twigs fell out of her messy hair.

"And you tripped over his feet as you were running to Glorybee?" Oscar wrote on his little notepad.

Anxiously, I paced back and forth, getting a couple of glimpses of Kenny. There was a crowd gathered outside of the shop. Isadora and Eloise watched the Karima sisters as they did their thing to prepare Kenny's departure from the doorway of A Charming Cure. I had to wonder if there was some sort of ceremonial procedure this community needed to do before they whisked him away.

"We will be back." Constance assured us as Patience tripped over Constance's feet. "Sister! Can you please stay at least one foot behind?"

"One foot behind." Patience repeated and opened her hands to span one foot between her and her sister.

There was a faint glow from Belur's bottle. Did he know? Did Belur really belong with him?

"I'm just a customer of June's." Adeline threw her hands up in the air. "I walked up and saw her," she pointed directly at Petunia and then at Gerald, "and him standing over *him*." She pointed back to Kenny.

"You didn't see anyone strange or suspicious running from the shop?" He questioned poor Adeline.

"No." She shook her head. Her pupils were dilated as she stared at Kenny. She couldn't take her eyes off him. Blindly she pointed toward Petunia and Gerald. "Just them."

Cough, cough. "Don't look at me." Gerald took his top hat off and held it to his chest, drumming his fingers on top of it. "We didn't do anything. I was comforting my sweet Petunia." He placed a hand on Petunia's shoulder.

"What about her?" Petunia glared at me. "It's *her* shop. *She* was the one asking around how to get in touch with him."

"Me?" My mouth dropped. "You think *I* killed him? When? I've been with you this whole time."

"Not all day." Petunia huffed, crossing her arms.

"I think it's time for you to go." Oscar shut his notebook. "Petunia and Gerald, I'll be filling out the report and dropping by to see you two tomorrow. You are free to go."

"I didn't do it." Petunia's teeth were clenched.

"Come on. Let Oscar figure this out." Gerald placed his hat back on his head and helped Petunia up.

"He's her *boyfriend*, Gerald." Petunia reminded him as if he didn't already know. "I want another officer on the case," She demanded, running over to Izzy. Petunia dropped to her knees with her hands clasped in the air. "Please, Izzy."

Gently, Izzy took her by the hands and pulled Petunia to her knees.

"It's out of my hands, dear." Izzy looked lovingly into Petunia's dark eyes.

"But you are the village. . ." Petunia dropped her hands when she realized that Izzy was no longer in charge. Slowly she turned back around. "June?"

Rushing to her side, I embraced her, crow and all.

"I know you couldn't have done this. Just like I didn't do it." My intuition told me something wasn't right. "Oscar will figure all of this out."

Out of nowhere, the old Two Sisters and A Funeral ambulance roared down the street, lights flashing and horn blaring as if nobody saw them.

"Outta the way." Constance pushed the gurney through the crowd. "Got a dead body we need to get."

"Yep, body we need to get to." Patience kept her eye on the prize.

I looked out the shop windows. Every single spiritualist had moved from the smudging ceremony circle to the front of A Charming Cure. Faith's smug smile caught my eye. Our eyes locked.

"Told ya." A smile crossed her face as she mouthed those two little words before she rotated on the balls of her feet and sashayed toward Wicked Goods.

Told me what? My hands began to sweat, and my face felt flush.

"June?"

I heard someone call my name, but I couldn't focus on anything but Faith's words, *"told ya"*.

Instantly my mind flooded with her words, *you will regret trying to tell me how to be a clairaudient.*

What did she mean by 'regret'? What did she mean by 'told ya'?

"June?" Oscar grabbed my arm. "You need to take a seat before you pass out."

Feeling a little bit like a zombie, my eyes lowered to Kenny's body as I walked past him to a stool to sit on. My intuition tugged in the pit of my stomach. This was not a coincidental murder.

Once the sisters had collected Kenny, Petunia and Gerald left. Adeline stood hunched in the corner. I swear I could hear the chattering of her teeth. She looked so scared. Or maybe it was my own teeth. Either way, the smell of death hung in the air like a heavy wool blanket.

I told Adeline to stop by in the morning, not asking her why she was here tonight. Reluctantly she agreed and left, but not without leaving me sick to my stomach.

Every time I got near her and Petunia, something told me everything was off with the world. But what? Why those two?

"Are you okay?" Oscar locked the door behind everyone.

"No." I ran my hands along and under the counter to find my all-important stress relief, Ding Dongs, but there were none there. "Damn! I'm out of Ding Dongs! June's Gem isn't going to cut it."

I made a mental note to drive into Locust Grove tomorrow for a Piggly Wiggly run and stock up on my delicious treats.

"You know I'm going to have to ask you some serious questions." Oscar lowered his big blue eyes, and I saw a seriousness that I didn't like. "It seems that asked a lot of villagers how to get in touch with Kenny. Then he showed up dead in your shop."

"I know how it looks." I buried my head in my hands. "But I didn't do it."

"What did you want with him?" Oscar pulled out his little notepad.

"Are you interrogating me?" I stumbled back and caught the wall behind me. I felt faint, and had a history of fainting.

"I told you that I needed to question you." He sat the pad on the counter, and then helped me sit on the stool Petunia vacated earlier, making me feel like I was in the hot seat. "I'm the sheriff. I have to ask these questions."

"All I know is I saw Kenny running toward A Charming Cure when Petunia was throwing her hissy fit about me being named the new village president."

"You saw him?" Oscar stared at me as if he didn't believe me. "June, he had been dead minutes before that, meaning there was no way you saw him."

"Seriously, are you interrogating me?"

"Not without her lawyer!" Mac McGurtle burst through the door with briefcase in hand. "I'm the village president's attorney. I need to speak with my client."

Village president? I'd forgotten about that.

Mac pushed his black-rimmed glasses up on his large nose with his thick little fingers, not taking his eyes off Oscar.

"Is my client under arrest?" Mac's briefcase made a thud when he sat it on the counter.

Meow, meow. Mr. Prince Charming danced around.

There was something else going on. Madame Torres glowed from the bottom of my bag and Belur illuminated from the shelf.

Oscar looked around and shook his head.

"Fine." Mac took him by the elbow. "If you'd kindly leave while I discuss the events of the night with my client."

Oscar strained his neck trying to look back at me, but Mac kept him walking toward the door.

"Here is my card." Mac handed his business card to Oscar. "If you should need any more assistance or contact with my client, please call me, not her."

Reluctantly Oscar took the card.

"Oh, and as of right now," Mac pointed between Oscar and me, "you two are no longer a

couple."

Chapter Ten

Meowl, meooowl. Mr. Prince Charming pranced around on my bed and finally settled on my pillow. *Meooooowl.* His paw landed on my tear-stained cheek.

I could never have imagined what had happened today. First, I got a crazy genie lamp. Second, I was named the new village president. Third, Kenny was found dead on my shop floor. Fourth, my relationship with Oscar was over, and fifth, my shop was closed until further notice.

"I told you all this was trouble." Madame Torres appeared in her globe. Sitting on the table, she filled the room with a warm brown glow. I was sure she'd picked the tone to match my somber mood.

"I don't want to hear 'I told you so.'" I rolled her to the other side so I didn't have to look at her. "I want to hear solutions. Mainly, how to get my name cleared and Oscar back."

Rolling her over didn't help. Belur was sitting on the dresser across the room from Madame Torres. I didn't have the energy to referee them.

"Your wish is my command," Belur belted out from the bottle. His voice trembled.

"Belur?" I propped myself up on my elbows. "Is there something you need to tell me?"

"I can't stand that ball of fur sitting on your table." The bottle shook, tipping side-to-side as if walking itself to the far end of the dresser. "The further away I am from *her*, the better."

"You are going to have to find a way to get along. Especially now, since we are in this big mess and your master is dead." I whispered the last part because I hadn't told him about Kenny. I assumed he didn't know because he hadn't mentioned it. "Wait!"

I jump to my feet.

"Did you see what happened last night at my shop?" I took his bottle in my hand and uncorked the top, hoping he'd pop out.

Nothing.

"Hey?" I held the bottle upside down and shook it. "Come out of there." I demanded.

Nothing.

"Oh, Belur." I put the top back on and sat him back on the dresser. "I wish I knew how to use a genie."

Meow. Mr. Prince Charming nudged me.

"You are right." I glanced at the clock. "Since we have nothing to do all day, we can run into Locust Grove to stock up on some Ding Dongs."

I bet I wouldn't be as stressed if I had a treat to snack on.

Mr. Prince Charming jumped off the bed as I searched for my sweats.

"I know." I smiled, looking down at him doing figure eights around my ankles, letting me know that everything would work out. "I hope it all does. But this time… I looked out the bedroom window and into Whispering Falls. "I think we are in big trouble."

I've been in a pickle or two, but no one was ever found dead in my shop before with no way to explain it.

Luckily, I had grabbed Belur before Oscar told Mac I wasn't going to be able to use the shop until further notice. I wasn't sure if it was Oscar's way of being in charge of me during this time or not, but Mac made it loud and clear we were not allowed to see each other during this investigation.

"Just where do you think you're going?" Mac McGurtle stood outside of my cottage door as soon as I opened it.

"I'm going to Locust Grove to the Piggly Wiggly." I looked down in my bag, moving Madame Torres over to fetch the Green Machine keys. "I need some Ding Dongs."

"I'm going with you." He didn't ask me—he told me. "We have some things to discuss. Some things about a bird and classes for level twenty-eight."

There wasn't going to be any arguing with Mac. I had learned that a long time ago. Mac was our neighbor in Locust Grove. He was always in our business and watched over me like a hawk after Darla died. Little did I know, the village council had placed him next door to keep us safe and sound from any dark spiritualist trying to find us. My father was killed, and his killer hadn't been caught. Once I moved to Whispering Falls and found out I had inherited my father's spiritual abilities, Mac had informed me why he was so nosy all those years.

"Fine, hop in." I unlocked the driver's side door of my old green '88 El Camino, and leaned across the cracked leather seats to unlock his door. Mr. Prince Charming perched on the headrest behind me as he always does. "Hold on!"

I put the Green Machine in gear and floored it. Mac grabbed the handle of the door, holding on for dear life.

I rubbed the dash as we made a mad dash out of Whispering Falls. "Still purrs like a baby."

I tried not to look in my rearview mirror as Whispering Falls got smaller and smaller. I never went anywhere without telling Oscar. With one hand on the wheel, I placed my other hand on my heart. It ached for him.

"I'm sorry, June." Mac's knuckles were white. He was gripping the door handle so hard. "But this isn't looking good. The evidence is mounting against you."

"Like what?" Sarcasm dripped from my lips. I had an ironclad alibi. "I was at the smudging ceremony the entire time."

"Not necessarily." He must have been getting brave since he let go of the door and slightly turned to face me.

"As village president, you automatically get powers that you will have to learn to control."

"Is that why Petunia was so mad?" I heard her say a million times how she wished she had more powers than talking to spirit animals.

He nodded. "She was next in line before Izzy figured out you inherited your father's ability."

It all made sense now why she was so mad.

"What about her?" It wouldn't have been impossible for her to have killed the Kenny "She was standing in the door of my shop. She could've killed him."

"Gerald said they tripped over his feet, they were hanging out the door." Mac pulled out his notepad and started to write some things down. But she could have done it. "My old mind isn't good for remembering things like it used to be."

I smiled. I wasn't sure how old Mac was, but he sure didn't look like he had aged.

"Now," He clicked the pen, "tell me everything that happened yesterday."

"I had customers and potions to make. I have a list of the potions I did make." I eased the Green Machine around the curvy road that led to Locust Grove. "I went to Wicked Good to talk to Faith about her predictions being wrong."

"Hmmm." He scribbled something down.

"What?"

"She can go on our suspect list." He looked over, pushing his big-rimmed glasses up on his nose.

"Faith wouldn't hurt a fly." I bit my lip, wondering if I should tell him I gave Faith a little Mugwort to help her hone her spiritual gift. Nah!

"Spiritualists don't like to be called out for a bad job." He said.

He was right. I'd never intended to hurt her feelings. I just want her be successful. Over the past few months, I had seen some spiritualists try to make their way in Whispering Falls, only to fail. Would she get back at me by framing me for murder? After all, I did just save her life a few months ago.

I shook the thought from my head. "I saw Petunia chasing that ostrich down the street."

"Yes, yes." He shuffled a few papers around, some spilling on the floorboard. "Here."

He held up a piece of paper with his chicken scribbles on it.

"She said that you were very suspicious of the ostrich. And you asked a lot of questions. It says here that you hindered her from catching the bird by trying to pluck a feather."

"And that's a crime?" I shrugged. "It had very pretty feathers."

"It is, since the bird seemed to have been kidnapped."

"You mean birdnapped." I couldn't help but laugh. If I didn't laugh at myself, I'd go crazy.

Mac glared at me, not amused at my joke. "The lock on his cage was cut with potion cutters." He ran his finger along the paper as he read her claim. "You can't deny the special cut they make."

He was right. I rarely used potion cutters, but I had them. They were intended for cutting thick potions that were meant to be eaten. I specialized in the liquid potions.

"Automatically, they are mine?" I couldn't remember the last time I used them. "I bet mine are still hanging on the hook."

"Nope." He said. I shot him a look and slammed on the breaks. "I checked, and so did Oscar."

Smacking the palms of my hands on the steering wheel, I glanced up as tears burned my eyes.

"Oh my," I gasped, glancing out the window, noticing we had stopped right in front of my old house in Locust Grove. There was a little girl sitting on the front steps in the exact place I used to sit. "I'd give anything to be a little girl again."

Mac rested his hand on my shoulder. Giving it a squeeze, he encouraged me. "June, we will figure this out. I know you didn't do it."

At that moment, I wished I could break the spiritual rule that would let spiritualists read other spiritualists. Then they'd see I didn't do it.

In silence, we drove to the Piggly Wiggly.

"I'll wait in the car." Mac said and continued to write things I had mentioned down in the notebook. It made me a little concerned he said his memory wasn't as good as it used to be, but I believed in him. He had always kept me safe, along with Mr. Prince Charming and my bracelet.

My intuition told me I was going to be safe, but I had to clear my own name. But how?

Chapter Eleven

Aisle five, aisle five, I thought as I headed straight for the Ding Dongs. I knew exactly where they were. I'd been going to that Piggly Wiggly aisle for as far back as I could remember.

It was Oscar who had gotten me hooked on the darn cupcakes. Oscar's uncle always had the best junk food, whereas Darla refused to allow the 'poison chemicals' in the house, much less put them in our bodies.

I used to sneak out and meet Oscar under the big oak tree on the far side of his house, out of view of Darla in case she looked outside, and we'd eat an entire box. I guess I should clarify, I'd eat an entire box while Oscar laughed.

"Stop it," I whispered. I had to get Oscar and the good times out of my head or I'd go crazy. "Need Ding Dongs, need Ding Dongs." I ran my finger down the aisle where they always sat, but the shelf was empty.

"Did you say Ding Dongs?" The guy in the green Piggly Wiggly employee shirt asked.

"Yes." Frantically I rushed up and down the aisle to see where they had moved them.

"You aren't going to find any. They stopped making them."

"You are joking, right?" I stopped dead in my tracks and searched his pimply teenage face. He was wrong. He was teasing me. My gut tugged, telling me he wasn't wrong, but my head told me he was. "You are a liar!"

"Whoa." A woman's voice called out from behind me. "June?"

"You are crazy, lady." The kid pointed at me before he walked away.

"Are you okay?" Adeline was standing in front of me. Her mouth gaped open.

"No. No. Nothing is okay." I threw my hands up in the air and burst out crying.

"Come on." She wrapped her arms around me and ushered me thru the swinging doors that read 'Employees Only'. "Clear out. Emergency." She told the employees to leave.

"Can you do that?" I questioned her as she placed me in a chair at the table where the employees had been eating. My stomach growled looking at their peanut butter and jelly sandwiches.

Another person walked in.

"I said leave!" She pointed toward the door. "Tell Brady to order pizza for everyone."

The employee smiled, walking out to leave us alone.

"Brady is the cashier manager today." She smiled, lifting her hands in the air. "You have A Charming Cure, I have the Piggly Wiggly."

"You are the owner?" Good. I had the right person who could answer my Ding Dong dilemma. "Then you can tell me---where are the Ding Dongs? They have been in aisle five for as far back as I can recall."

"They aren't making them anymore. We had to do away with the entire display." There was a sadness in her voice and eyes. "I'm so sorry. Be glad that you have those delicious treats you gave me that are similar to them. I'm losing money left and right since the supplier stopped all production."

"I know." I shuffled my foot. "My friend at Wicked Good Bakery in Whispering Falls makes them. But there's just something about the real thing and unwrapping that foil."

"This can be a good thing. Maybe you can do something different to help out with stress." She stood up and put her hands together in a praying position. "I was going to check on you today after what happened last night."

"Oh, yeah." Kenny's dead body was tattooed on my brain. "Last night."

"Do they know what happened to him?" She leaned against the table.

"He was murdered, but the autopsy isn't back yet." I made a mental note to make a quick visit to Two Sisters and a Funeral. Surely the results from his autopsy were back by now.

"I know you didn't do it. You have to find a better way to soothe that stress of yours." She bowed with her hands still in the clasped position. "I really think you should join me in yoga."

Yoga? Chocolate? Weighing the two, I think chocolate wins.

"I'll think about it." I straightened my shirt. "I'm going to go. Thanks so much for your help."

"Anytime." Adeline made it to the door before me and opened it. "It feels good to help you out instead of the other way around."

"Technically, you just killed my one and only bad habit." I bit my lip trying to figure out how I was going to get my hands on some Ding Dongs. "I'll let you know about the yoga thingy."

Pish. There was no way I was going to do that meditating crap when all I needed was a Ding Dong.

"Hi," Adeline's voice rose to a high-pitched squeal when a sandy blond-haired guy greeted us.

*Hmm...*Was this why single women went to the grocery store? To find a man? No wonder the produce section was so popular.

He bent down and gave Adeline a kiss to remember. She melted right into him, forgetting all about me and my dilemma.

"I'm sorry." Adeline's face was rosy red as she wiped her mouth with the back of her hand, and then rubbed her hand down the hot, hunky man. "George, this is June. The owner of..."

"A Charming Cure." He smiled and nodded. George stuck his hand out. We shook. "It's great to meet the face behind the name. My Adeline has told me all about you."

"It's nice to meet you." I pointed toward the door. "I really need to get going."

"Okay." Adeline tucked her arms in the crook of his elbow, locking her hands. Her shoulders rolled up. "I'll check back with you about yoga."

"You aren't trying to get her to do yoga are you?" By the sound of George's voice, she must be trying to get him to go with her.

"I'll think about it." George reminded me of how I had to find a new stress relief, putting a bitter taste back in my mouth. "I'll see you later." I eyed her suspiciously, my gut tugged and I fiddled with my fingers.

Angrily, I stomped back to the Green Machine. Mac had rolled down the window and was drumming his fingers on the windowsill.

"Where have you been?" Hastily he rolled the window back up.

"You aren't going to believe this." I let out a big sigh. "They are no longer making Ding Dongs, the end of an era and the end of sanity for me."

"You better find something and quick." Mac's voice sent chills up my spine. "Wicked Goods was robbed last night."

"Oh, no." I gasped. "Do they think the killer broke in there?"

"They think *you* did." Mac opened his damn notebook. "The only thing they took," he looked up, his eyes hollow, "were June's Gems."

Instantly, Adeline's face hit my mind's eye like a ton of bricks. My gut curled in knots. My instincts told me her name was written all over this. Not only did she get the June's Gems for her boyfriend, but she was also standing there last night when Petunia and Gerald stumbled across Kenny. Plus, she'd do anything to keep that boyfriend of hers. After all, all she wanted the first time she came into A Charming Cure was a potion to help in the relationship department. All I gave her was a box of June's Gems without a potion.

Did Kenny see her stealing from Wicked Good and try to stop her, and she killed him?

"What?" Mac questioned me. "Tell me what you are thinking. I need the truth June."

"The truth is…" I stopped, and looked at the front of the Piggly Wiggly. Adeline was standing next to the sliding doors, waving her fingers in the air as she said bye to me.

I put the car in drive.

"The truth is I'm innocent." With my eyes ahead of me, I decided to keep my intuitive claims about Adeline private. I had a lot of questions that needed to be answered, and I was going to find out the answers for myself.

"Ohmmmm…" I hummed.

"What?" Mac's nose twitched, and he had a peculiar look on his face.

"Nothing." I inhaled what was supposed to be fresh air to help with the Zen, but it smelled like the ole Green Machine. Practicing yoga just might be what I needed to get to the truth about who

killed Kenny and broke into Wicked Good.

Chapter Twelve

"Am not!" Belur screamed. He could be heard arguing with Madame Torres even with the door shut and a couch pillow over my head.

"Are too!" Madame Torres knew how to get under Belur's skin when she told him he was a fat blob with no real powers.

"Am not!"

"Yep you are!" She was confident in her argument and he really couldn't do anything but what he was told. "You can only grant wishes. Not like me. I can see exactly what is going to happen to people, and show June pictures of things going on around her."

Hiss, hiss. Mr. Prince Charming darted out of the bedroom and jumped on the couch. He rubbed his body against my hand that was holding the pillow in place.

I didn't have the energy to play referee between them.

Pulling the pillow off my head, I sat up and smoothed my hair before I reached down and patted Mr. Prince Charming.

"I know this is going to protect me, but I wish I could have a break in the murder. Something." I bit my lip trying to listen to my instincts, but nothing was coming. "Come on."

The knock at the door startled me. It was loud and demanding.

Meow, meow. Mr. Prince Charming jumped up on the kitchen counter and stood on the window seal looking out.

Slowly I walked to the door, hoping it was Oscar, but not here to arrest me.

"What a fine mess the village president has gotten herself into." Aunt Helena swept past me, as her long red-pointy fingernail tweaked my nose. Her long black cloak created a breeze that sent chills up my spine.

My Great Aunt Helena was my father's aunt and the Dean of Hidden Hall A Spiritualist University. She was the last person I wanted to see. I'm sure I had disappointed her.

"Come on in," I sarcastically muttered while shutting the door. "Can I get you something to drink?"

Her cloak flew open, revealing a couple of to-go cups from The Gathering Grove and a brown bag. The goodies scent wafted through the room, making my stomach growl.

"I thought I'd stop by and bring you some food." Her eyes roamed up and down my body. "I can see that you haven't slept or eaten."

Opening the cupboard door, I pulled out two small plates and sat them on the small kitchen table. "Being accused of murder and now theft, and losing my boyfriend, leaves me with little appetite." I opened the bag after she handed it to me. Suddenly I was starving. I took a big bite of one of the blueberry muffins. "Mmmm." I closed my eyes, relaxing for the first time in twenty-four hours.

Patience and Constance Karmina popped into my head.

Which meant I needed to plan a little visit to Two Sisters and a Funeral Home. Their image was quickly replaced with Madame Torres.

"I'll be right back." I dropped the muffin back on the plate and rushed to the bedroom, quickly glancing back at Aunt Helena who was watching every single move I made. With a slight smile, I disappeared into the room. "You two stop it," I whispered, looking back and forth between the two. "My Aunt can't know about Belur, so stop fighting. I will deal with you when she leaves. Got it?"

Belur was in his bottle, but it was glowing an omescent purple that shut off as soon as I said to stop, but Madame Torres was a different story. Why on earth did I think she was going to cooperate?

While walking over to her to give her a scolding, I noticed it wasn't Madame Torres at all. I picked the crystal ball up to get a closer look.

"Adeline?" My eyes grew big and bright. Her hands were folded in her cross-legged lap, her eyes shut. She opened them and stared directly at me as if she knew she was in my crystal ball. Pulling her legs outstretched in front of her, she lifted her chest and torso, her hands above her head, and with one big exhale she bent forward leading with her chest, laying completely flat against her legs. "Why are you showing me this?" I asked Madame Torres, but she shut off.

With a heavy sigh, I went back to find Aunt Helena happily sipping her tea and eating her muffin.

"Find what you were looking for?" She questioned arrogantly.

"I must've left my Magical Cures Potion book at the shop." I lied, not looking at her. "I have a question about level twenty-eight."

"That is one reason I am here." Her long pinky finger shot straight up in the air as she tipped the cup to her lips. After a quick sip, she politely snickered, "You really shouldn't be doing any sort of the potions from level twenty-eight until you come back and take the Telekinesis course."

That was one spiritual gift I wanted to forget.

"That..."I grumbled, thinking my day had gone from bad to worse. "Are you telling me that wasn't a one-time gig?"

"I'm afraid not." Gracefully, Aunt Helena stood up, the hem of her cloak floated to the floor.

I would kill for a Ding Dong. I thought, remembering how I first learned I had the spiritual gift of Telekinesis. A time I'd like to forget. It was when I was a student at Hidden Hall, and in a very sticky situation.

"It's very important for you to learn how to control your gift." She flung the cloak perfectly over her left shoulder. "Especially now that you are the village president." She twirled her long finger in front of my face. "This is not the picture of a strong village president. Now get in there, get that loony crystal ball of yours, demand that pitiful sheriff give you back your shop, and lead this community into finding out who killed that poor Native American."

Like a good soldier, I straightened up and felt a little bit of confidence; not much, but some.

"You are a Heal, and no Heal ever cowers away from sticky situations." Her eyes narrowed, casting a dark shadow down her face. In an instant she was gone.

Hiss, hiss. Mr. Prince Charming arched his back, running through the puff of smoke she left behind.

"Why couldn't I have that fabulous spiritual gift?" I looked at him as he darted around my ankles.

She was right; I had to go into town as if nothing was bothering me. The more I stayed away, the guiltier I looked. At least that how it was on TV.

Quickly, I put on some other clothes that were a little more presentable then the sweat pants, grabbed Madame Torres, and shoved her deep in my bag before Mr. Prince

Charming and I headed down the hill towards Whispering Falls.

With Two Sisters and A Funeral in my sights, I ventured in that direction. It was good to see the town was filled with customers going from shop to shop.

"June, it's just awful that they think you did something to Kenny." Chandra Shango rushed outside of A Cleansing Spirit Spa. "He was shady." She tucked the ends of her short raspberry colored hair under the edge of her green turban before she plucked a few of the dead flowers from the window boxes that made her display windows pop. "What kind of person 'blows in with the wind and out with the breeze?'" She rolled her soft hazel eyes.

"Thank you so much for your support." Gently, I reached out and took her hand. Immediately she flipped it over and took a fast glance at my palm. I pulled it away. There was a lot going on inside of me. I didn't want to take a chance of Chandra seeing something. I curled my hand into a fist and placed it on my heart "I'm not going to let that stop me from serving as village president."

"What about that?" She pointed toward A Charming Cure, which was the shop next to hers. A big yellow piece of paper was stuck on the front window, completely covering up my cute potion display table.

"Closed until further notice?" My mouth dropped. He told me I had to close for a day. . .but until further notice? "We will see about that!"

I stormed down the street to take care of business at Two Sisters.

"Slow down," Madame Torres chirped from the bottom of my bag. "I'm getting motion sickness."

I ducked to the side of the moss-covered shop so no one would see me.

I reached in and pulled her out, holding her in the palm of my hands.

"Show me Adeline," I demanded.

Madame Torres knew I meant business. She didn't fuss as she showed me the inside of the Piggly Wiggly where Adeline was in the office having a little smooch session with her boyfriend.

"Ugh," I looked away, trying to give Adeline privacy, but looked back when a small cough came from Madame Torres. Adeline's boyfriend walked out of the office, but another guy emerged from the closet. He was not facing me, he was facing Adeline. I squinted trying to read her lips, which I couldn't do. By the way she was shaking her hands in the air, and gritting her teeth I could tell she wasn't happy.

I put Madame Torres back in my bag before I crossed the street. I didn't want to walk in front of Wicked Good. I hadn't seen Raven since I had been accused of robbing the bakery. They could just raid my cottage and see that I didn't.

"How is everything going?" Bella was cleaning the windows on the outside of her shop. "I'm sure you heard about the June's Gems being stolen." I shuffled my feet. "Oscar shut down my shop."

"June, I'm so sorry." There was sadness in her eyes. "Have you talked to Eloise?"

"No." I shook my head. "She was probably the first person Oscar went to since she was his aunt. Putting her in the middle isn't an option."

"You'd be surprised." Bella swiped the window with the cloth, rubbing off all of the cleaner. "Even though she is his aunt, she was also your mom's best friend. You need to reach out to her during your time of need."

"What does that mean?" I asked her. She definitely knows something, but what? I still had a lot of learning to do within this community.

"You are the village president now." Bella reminded me. "You should get to know all of the citizens in the community."

She was right. If none of this had ever happened, I would be making my rounds, visiting with all the community shop owners and healers in the village. Eloise was the one spiritualist that walked through the village in the wee hours of the morning with her incense, cleansing Whispering Falls on a daily basis. Many times, I would wake up before the rooster crowed, and see Eloise, along with Izzy, walking the streets for the morning cleanse.

"I think I'll do that, starting with the Karima sisters." I smiled at Bella, realizing she was helping me with my new role.

"Good idea." Bella disappeared back into her shop, followed by a few customers.

Mr. Prince Charming darted ahead and up the big concrete steps that lead to the front stain-glass doors of Two Sisters and A Funeral. I pushed the door open.

I had never been to visit the Karima sisters, but I figured it was like any other funeral home.

"Come on." I gestured for Mr. Prince Charming, but he sat on the stoop dragging his tail. He stared at me for a brief second before he darted down the porch. "Chicken."

There was something eerie about being in a place where there was a dead body, much less two. One of them I was accused of putting there.

The long wide hallway was dark. The walls were draped in long deep-red fabric that hung from ceiling to floor. Definitely, a designing style I had never seen. The pale yellow carpet with small red diamond designs lined the floors. Four large heavy ornamental wooden doors, two on each side, were shut. The massive staircase at the end opened up to a wraparound balcony.

"I'm not listening to you," Patience Karima's voice drifted through the air. "I don't care what you have to say so be quiet. I have a job to do."

Using my gift of instincts, and the fact I have ears, I followed the sound of her voice to the second door. Holding my breath, I put my ear to the door to see who she was talking to.

"If Constance comes back here and discovers you, we will both be in trouble."

Cling, clank, cling. The sound of something hitting a metal tray echoed through the crack at the bottom of the door. I lay down on the carpet and looked through the crack. The only feet I saw were Patience's feet. I would know those black slip-on shoes anywhere. All the elderly people that came to A Dose of Darla in my old flea market days wore those. They said they were the most comfortable shoes. Still, I'd rather go for a little fashion, but I guess it didn't matter to Patience's clients what she wore. They were all dead.

A feather floated next to her foot, and then another one.

Ostrich! Didn't Oscar say the ostrich from the strays that Petunia was keeping was missing?

I jumped up and turned the knob, busting through the door. If I could get the ostrich back, it would be one less crime I had to solve that I was being accused of committing.

"Caught ya!" I screamed, but came to an abrupt stop when Patience was leaning over Kenny's body with a tube going in one end and another coming out the other.

"June Heal!" Patience dropped the scalpel from her hand. It landed like a meat cleaver in her foot. "Ouch!" She hopped around on one foot as she tried to pull the knife out.

She went one way around the embalming table while I tried to cut her off the other way. Kenny's headdress was losing feathers left and right, and losing them fast. They fluttered through the air as our bodies created a lot of wind.

"Stop!" I put my hands out in front of me for Patience to stand still. "Let me help you."

She squeezed her little beady eyes shut, and huffed. The hot air coming out of her nose, fogged up her glass. "Ow, ow. Ow!" She screamed as I pulled the knife out of her shoe.

"Let me see your foot!" I demanded, following her hobbling body to the chair in the corner. I tried not to look at the dead guy, but it was difficult. He looked as if he was sleeping.

Patience peeled off her compression therapy leggings, revealing a tiny spot on the top of her foot.

"Help!" Patience screamed as though she were being killed. "Help me!"

I threw my hand over her mouth. "What is wrong with you? Stop screaming."

"If you think you are going to put me on that table like you did him, you are crazy!" She stuttered and pointed, "You're crazy!"

"Patience, I didn't kill him and you know that." I stood back and crossed my arms, watching her with cautious eyes. "You know I didn't don't you?"

"Constance will be back soon and I have to get my job done." With her shoe off, she got up and staggered across the floor to her workstation as if she had been stabbed nearly to death. "You'd better leave."

"Who were you talking to Constance?" I came here for some answers, but I didn't know what answers those were. I was only going on my instincts. "Come on Constance, I won't tell anyone."

She placed her hands on the arm of the body as if he were still alive. "I have a job to do. And another one is waiting." She referred to the out of town body they had gotten.

"Patience, aren't you tired of living under Constance's rules?" I asked, trying to get her to defy whatever she was scared of. Constance always seemed to tell Patience what to do and when to do it. And if Patience had some sort of freedom, she might know something that could help me out.

Patience grabbed her foot and scrunched up her face like an old prune as if she were in all sorts of pain.

"Why don't you come by the shop and I will get you some medicine for that?" I pointed to her little cut.

She bit her lip and shook her head no.

"Okay." I walked over to the door and turned around, "If you change your mind, you know where to find me."

She didn't look up as I left the room. I shut the door behind me. There was a lot going on within these funeral home walls. I had to come back when I could stay longer. But those bodies gave me the heebie jeebies.

I was anxious to rip that sign off the door of the shop. It was high time to open A Charming Cure, whether Oscar liked it or not.

I stood at the top of the steps of Two Sisters and A Funeral, peering down Main Street at all the shops and customers. I *was* the village president. I had to find a way to get answers. Opening my shop would give me the relaxation I needed to kick my intuition into gear. I started down the first step and stopped.

Picking a feather up off the step, I held it up in the sunlight, wondering how many more feathers Kenny was going to lose until he was laid to rest. More importantly, my gut told me these feathers meant something. But what?

Chapter Thirteen

"I dare you to think that you can just close my shop," I muttered, ripping the police line tape off the front gate of A Charming Cure. The Police Station looked dark, but I was sure Oscar watching nervously as I wadded the yellow tape up and threw it in the street. "I'll show you who's boss."

Rowr! Mr. Prince Charming batted at the dangling tape.

I stomped up to the door and marched in before I let this little ole mix of a murder stop me from my job. I was innocent and I was going to prove it.

Rolling up my sleeves, I flipped the light switch on. All of the little table lamps, sconces, and overhead cane lights illuminated, bringing a soft, inviting glow into the shop. The bottles on the tables sparkled, showing off their magical cures inside.

A warm fuzzy feeling came over me, as it always did when I was in the store. My intuition told me everything was going to be fine.

Meow, meow. Mr. Prince Charming jumped on the counter. I set my bag next to him and gave him a nice long rub down his back. He purred and arched his back with delight.

"You are going to have to leave this instance, Ms. Heal." The baritone voice growled from behind. "You are violating police procedure, and I can put you in jail for this."

The man stood in the entrance of A Charming Cure tapping the police baton in the palm of his hand.

"Who are you?" I asked. "I mean, I know you are a police officer by the outfit and all. But what do you have to do with Whispering Falls and my shop?"

"You will have to see the Order of Elders for the answers you are seeking." He stepped inside the shop. "This is a police investigation and I'm in charge."

"He wasn't found dead *in* my shop," I reminded him. I crossed my arms and tried to hone into my intuition. Was he who he said he was? And where was Oscar?

"Ms. Heal, everyone knows that the perimeter of the crime scene is blocked off. And this," he circled his hands in the air, "is considered the perimeter and part of the crime scene. I told all of this to Mr. McGurtle and he should have told you."

"He did, but that was yesterday." I played stupid. "And what is that about an Order of Elders?"

I flipped to the appendix in the back of the Magical Cures Book to see if there was anything at all about this order, but there wasn't.

"When a village president is involved in a crime, the Order of Elders then step in." He picked up a bottle of potion for hair, which he definitely didn't need. He had the thickest head of unruly black hair I had ever seen. "You are in big trouble, Ms. Heal. So I suggest you get in contact with the Order as quickly as possible."

"How do I do that?" *Big trouble?* I swallowed hard because that didn't sound good at all.

"I do not know that." He set the bottle back down and started to tap the baton again.

"Where is Oscar?" I gathered some of the items I needed at my house to create a makeshift shop just in case I needed to make a potion. "I would like to talk to him about all of this before I leave you here."

I picked up the Magical Cure Book and held it tight. It wasn't that I didn't believe everything he was saying, but it was strange no one, including Mr. McGurtle, had told me this information.

"He is no longer on the case." He held the door wide open, as if for me to walk through. "He has been transferred for the time being."

Transferred? My mind went cloudy. I grasped the corners of the book. The room spun in circles and then up and down. I tried to take a couple of deep breaths, but then everything went black.

Chapter Fourteen

"Oh, dear." The sweet angelic voice rang in my ears. "Do you think she's all right?"

"She better be all right." Another unfamiliar voice broke with huskiness.

"I honestly can't believe she's the new village president of Whispering Falls." The third unknown voice was much calmer. "It's such a wonderful community. I hope it doesn't start going downhill."

"It will all be fine," Eloise said in a hushed whisper. "June is wonderful. She has to get used to all the magic. She only found out about all of this a few years ago. Unlike us. We've been doing this all our lives."

Open, open. I begged my eyes to open. My lids felt heavy as if there were dollar-sized coins taped on them.

"Gandalf said she fainted when he told her that Oscar had been transferred." The angelic voice whispered. "Young love."

"Who cares about love when we are in crisis mode?"

"Now, now." Eloise tried to settle down the feisty one. "Let's be calm so we can figure this mess out."

"Look," the sweet voice gasped, "her eyes are fluttering."

Fluttering? Please open, please open. I continued to will my lashes to pop open.

I tried to focus on the blurry images as the sound of footsteps gathered around me.

"I told you," she confirmed. "June?"

"Move, let Eloise try." The husky voice was patronizing. "She knows her. You will only freak her out more."

"June, dear?" Eloise had always been so comforting. "Mr. Prince Charming is here."

Mewl, mewl. The long tail wrapped around my neck as Mr. Prince Charming slowly dragged it across.

"I…" I stammered, "Oscar."

The last thing I remember was that man telling me that Oscar had been transferred. I didn't believe it. He would have found a way to say good-bye to me.

"Yes, June." Eloise sat down next to me. My eyes focused on her face, though I could tell I was in her tree house. I saw three other shadows around me that had not yet come into focus. But I knew they belonged to the three voices I did not recognize. "We can talk about Oscar when you are well."

"Has he been. . ." I looked deep into her emerald eyes and began to sob when I could see that Oscar was gone.

"June, he will be back when all of this is cleared up." Eloise swept her arms around me, practically lying on top of me. "He hated it so much he had to leave without a good-bye, but that is the way they do things around here when the village president finds herself in a sticky situation."

I turned away. The thought of Oscar having to be sent away was more than I could bear, and the fact I hadn't been without him since we were children didn't help matters.

"I told you Petunia was a much stronger candidate for the job." The deeper voice of a shadow moved away from me. Her footsteps were solid and loud.

I laid there for what seemed to be forever, but knew it was only a few minutes so my eyes could adjust. When I felt somewhat more myself, I propped up on my elbows to get a better look at what was going on around me.

Blinking my eyes, I did realize the three women I didn't know were sitting with their legs crossed in mid-air. Each one was older than the other.

"Hi," the little old woman with the sweet southern voice was suddenly hovering over me. She was no bigger than four feet tall with a small black pillbox hat nestled on top of her tight curled silver hair. The fox stole wrapped around her neck was perfectly attached to the collar of her black suit. She looked like she had class. "I'm Mary Lynn, one of the Elders, here to help you."

"Howdy!" Another shadow came into focus. A much younger, more hip woman floated next to Mary Lynn. Her one-piece black bodysuit was barely visible under her long leopard mink coat "I'm Mary Ellen. The fabulous Elder." She cackled aloud.

"I'm Mary Sue, the other one." The third and last Elder didn't move from her invisible chair in the air. "We make up the Order of Elders. We are all past village presidents of different communities. You have been accused of murder, and if you ask me, I am not sure you didn't do it."

"Mary Sue!" Mary Ellen and Mary Lynn shouted.

"Don't you mind her." Mary Lynn patted my hand and sat next to me. "Sometimes witches do deserve the ugly image of having warts on their noses when they act like Mary Sue."

"She's just an old coot!" Mary Ellen floated down, sticking her tongue out at Mary Sue. "Besides, we are here to get to the bottom of who killed poor Kenny."

"What about Oscar?" I sat up; Mr. Prince Charming jumped off the couch and darted out the front steps of the tree house. "I can't do anything without Oscar."

Eloise stepped up, her cloak creating a wind tunnel as she sat next to me on the other side. "Oscar wanted to tell you good-bye, but he wasn't allowed. He went to sorcery school early. He will be fine. Everything will be back to normal soon."

"First we have to take care of business." Mary Sue came down and stood next to the couch, her body casting a shadow over me. "Why did you want to get in touch with Kenny? Everyone in town seems to think you were desperate to talk to him. Then he shows up dead. Suspicious!" She pointed a finger at me and a spark flew from it.

I ducked, not sure if she was casting.

"Stop being so dramatic. You are going to scare the poor girl." Mary Ellen stood up, placing herself between Mary Sue and me. She planted her hands on her hips. "We know you didn't do it, but we don't know who did."

"That is why we are here." Mary Lynn stood up. There was a little rattle as she adjusted her suit skirt. "We will leave you to get some rest. We will be back later to ask some questions, but only when you feel well."

The Marys stood next to each other and with a flick of their hands, they disappeared.

"If I'd only known what Whispering Falls was all about, I doubt I would have come here to live." I sat with my face in my hands.

"That is no way to act." Eloise brought me a cup of tea from the kitchen. "We are here to help figure this out. Don't mind Mary Sue. She's the oldest and really she should retire. She's a softy at heart."

"They are fine." I took the cup from her and took a sip. "Thank you."

"Can you tell me why you wanted to see Kenny so bad?"

"This." I reached into my bag and pulled out Belur. Slowly I wiggled the cork off the top. Immediately a stream of purple fog filled the air and Belur stood in the middle.

"Your wish is my command, Master June." He bowed with his hands clasped in front of him.

"Kenny left that at my shop." I bit my lip waiting for Eloise's reaction.

"Oh, no." She shook her head. "A genie."

"And what is wrong with that?" Belur crossed his massive arms in front of him and tapped his toe. The bell on the pointy tip jingled with each tap.

"There's nothing wrong with it if you were in a different type of spiritualist community, but your type isn't allowed in Whispering Falls." She got up, walked over to the shelf of books and pulled down a binder that clearly read Whispering Falls By-Laws. She opened it and tapped a page, showing Belur. "See, right here."

"Why don't I have one of those?" That would have definitely come in handy when I decided to move here and take the village president position.

"Yours is coming," She confirmed. "You were just sworn in as the President."

"Why aren't I welcome?" Belur pushed his chin in the air, casting his eyes down on Eloise.

"Who doesn't want their wishes granted? If you got into the wrong hands, everything could go horribly wrong."

"See? That is why I needed to get in touch with him." I threw my hands in the air.

"Did you break into Wicked Good?"

"No!" I protested.

"What about the ostrich? Did you kidnap him?"

"Me? No." I knew I was going to have to spill the beans about the spell I gave Faith to drink. "I needed feathers from an ostrich for a potion."

"Who did you give Mugwort to?" Eloise asked. "Remember I was best friends with your mother and we always dabbled in that book. Besides, you aren't a level twenty-eight yet."

There weren't too many things I could keep from Eloise. She had known me since birth and she did sorta replace Darla when I moved back to Whispering Falls.

"Faith," I whispered.

"June!"

"She needed help with her skills and I thought a little bit of Mugwort wasn't going to hurt. So when I saw Petunia and *that* ostrich, it was a sign." I had to get the heat off me. "Did they find the bird?"

"No, as a matter of fact, they are searching your property and you can't go home." She walked over to the window and looked out into the woods. "You are going to have to stay here until further notice. And Izzy is interim village president until further notice."

"I guess I screwed up this time." I walked up behind her and looked out over the treetops and into the beautiful woods.

"You are right about one thing." She turned around and faced me. The lines between her eyes creased with worry. "No one can know about Belur. Not even the Marys."

Her words sent chills up my spine. There was something in her tone that confirmed that someone was putting all of these crimes on me. I still couldn't shake the facts. Faith and Petunia were both mad at me for various reasons. And it wouldn't be the first time that someone had murdered for revenge.

Chapter Fifteen

There were many things running through my head the entire night as I sat on Eloise's couch, not to mention the noises that were coming from outside. I wasn't use to sleeping in the woods, and neither was Mr. Prince Charming.

Mewwl, mewwl. He threw his head up in the air toward the sun that was shining in through the large windows of the den.

"What is it?" I asked him, wishing that for one second I could have Petunia's gift of communicating with the animals. Normally, I'd go to Petunia if I were in a situation where I needed to know what Mr. Prince Charming was thinking, but not now. Not today anyway.

Especially since she and I were both suspects in Kenny's murder, as well as her believing I stole the ostrich, which was insane.

Okay, maybe it wasn't too insane since I did need one of those feathers.

"Hear ye, hear ye," Faith's voice was a lot quieter than yesterday.

I rushed over to the door and out onto the porch to see if I could hear her better. Mr. Prince Charming darted out behind me. Immediately, he started his figure eights around my ankles, only this time he ran over to the steps and back again. He repeated this several times.

"Stop," I begged him as I tried to listen into the dawn air. The whipping wind and crackling branches made it hard to hear.

"The funeral service for our dearly departed Kenny will be held at Two Sisters. . ." Faith's voice trailed off, floating back again in spurts. Mr. Prince Charming darted down the stairs of Eloise's tree house and into the night.

"What? June Heal what?" I asked. Squinting I tried to see where Mr. Prince Charming ran off too.

Maybe I need to get closer to Whispering Falls to hear, and that is what he's trying to tell me. Without a second's delay, I ran in and grabbed my bag off the couch, and took off down the steps after him and closer to Whispering Falls. It would make sense that the paper wouldn't carry into the woods since it was for the community.

Carefully, I stepped out into the meadow where the Gathering Rock was situated between the village and the woods, and quickly ran behind the rock. I couldn't risk anyone seeing me since the Order of Elders told me to stay put at Eloise's house. Also from here, I'd be able to see if the fireflies were still out or if they had gone home. They would definitely tell Petunia they saw me if she asked.

"Tsk, tsk." Aunt Helena crossed the field as if the dawn air was carrying her, landing on her pointy-heeled shoes right in front of me. My bangs blew up as her long green cloak swooshed around her.

Hiss, hiss. Mr. Prince Charming ran off toward our home. I wanted to tell him to stop, but Aunt Helena knew I was up to something, only I couldn't tell her what because I didn't know.

"Oh shut up," She muttered in Mr. Prince Charming's direction. It was no secret there was no love lost between the two. In fact, she had been upset that the Village Council had appointed Mr. Prince Charming as my Fairy god-cat in the first place. He was always by my side and I loved him just the same.

I stood still as she walked around me, *slowly*, never taking her eyes off me. I waited with anticipation to what she was going to say.

"I'm assuming Eloise doesn't know that you have escaped?" She raised her hands in the air and a spark shot out of the tip of her fingers as her hands came back down and she pointed in Eloise's direction.

"It was unplanned." Which wasn't a lie. I didn't intend to follow Mr. Prince Charming into town. "I was trying to hear the morning news better since it was so faint at the tree house. Plus, Faith had said something about me."

"I wouldn't worry too much about Faith." Aunt Helena really liked Faith when we were at Hidden Hall. In fact, Faith was her favorite student. "She will come into her own gift, just as you did. And without the help of Mugwort." Her eyes were downcast on me.

"I had to do something." I threw my hands in the air. "She obviously didn't listen in clairaudience class."

"You *obviously* didn't listen when I told you you needed to come take a class for level twenty-eight." Her eyebrows dipped in a frown. "You won't get any better with your cures until you finish your schooling."

"What exactly does that mean?" There were times I felt everyone here had a common language that I was not a part of. I grew up with regular, old, run-of-the-mill people in a normal community, not a spiritualist one, and I think they forget that sometimes.

"It means you will not be able to do anymore cures than the ones you know. Being a spiritualist is just like any other craft, you have to keep learning June, or your skills will die."

Die? I studied Aunt Helena's face to see if she was bluffing or telling the truth, because death seemed a little harsh. Her face was still and serious.

"Now would probably be a good time to do that." At least it would get me out of here.

She threw her head back and roared with laughter. The birds scattered from the trees.

"Did you ask the three musketeers?" She brought her hand up to stifle her giggle.

"Who?"

"Mary Sue, Mopsey and Mopey." She waved her hands in the air. "Those three Marys." From the lack of respect she was giving them, I could tell she wasn't a big fan of them either.

"You mean Mary Sue, Mary Ellen and Mary Lynn?" I asked.

"You know good and well what I mean." She crossed her arms in disgust. "They shouldn't be the Order of Elders, but that's for another time. Have you discussed this with them? After all, you are banned until further notice."

I put my hands together and batted my eyes. "Can't you ask them for me? You are the Dean."

If I had to play the Dean's niece card, I would.

"Of course I will." She smiled, causing her eyes to narrow like a cat's. She wrapped her arm around me and her cloak followed. "When shall I expect you?"

There were a few things I needed to get done. First, I had to make a stop into Locust Grove and see Adeline. I had to do a little bit of snooping and I wanted to know who she was fighting with. Then I needed to go to Kenny's funeral.

I didn't know why I needed to go, but I did.

"How about this time tomorrow?"

"I'll be waiting." Her hands flew to her side and she vanished. Right into thin air.

"I wish I could disappear like that." I was green with envy at Aunt Helena's skills. Why couldn't I have those kinds of spiritual gifts instead of the whole intuition thing?

Chapter Sixteen

"Where are you?" I hissed into the air in a hushed whisper. Mr. Prince Charming didn't want to be anywhere near Aunt Helena. He darted off so fast when she showed up that I didn't see where he went. "Mr. Prince Charming." I ran my fingers along my wrist, wishing I had my charm bracelet. I could use a little luck right about now.

Off in the distance, closer to our house that sits on the hill overlooking Whispering Falls, a long white tail danced in the sunrise. He was heading straight toward our cottage, but why?

He knew I wasn't supposed to go anywhere near our home, but I knew he wasn't going to send me into danger.

Like a good Fairy goddaughter, I went where he was leading me and it was right in the front seat of the Green Machine.

"You are a stinker." I pushed the manual locks down, and then hunkered down and rubbed his back before he nestled in a ball on the dashboard. I couldn't risk anyone seeing me. Slowly, I raised my head and looked out the passenger window to see if I could see anyone in the house.

It was dark, but that didn't mean no one was there. "Now, how am I supposed to get this thing started without my keys?"

Tap, tap, tap.

I lay on the seat hoping whoever was tapping on the Green Machine window didn't see me, but obviously, they did.

Please don't see me, I thought with my eyes tightly shut.

"I can see you."

"Oscar?" I sat up and could feel the joy come back to my soul.

"Are you looking for these?" He dangled the keys off his finger, but looked around to see if anyone saw him. "Let me in." He motioned to the lock.

Without hesitation, I pulled the silver lock up and slid to the passenger side of the Green Machine.

"Did you see anyone in there?" He asked before he leaned over and took me into his arms.

"No." I pushed him back. "Are you going to arrest me?"

Fear and anxiety knotted inside my gut from the thought of the percussion of violating my parole set on me by the Order of Elders. Seeing him was probably worth it. A calmness washed over me as my intuition told me to trust him.

Meow, meow. Mr. Prince Charming wasn't too alarmed to see him either. He threw his back leg up in the air and began cleaning his fur.

"Let's get out of here first." Oscar put the keys in the ignition. Turning the old El Camino on, he eased out of town without anyone seeing us.

We rode in silence with our hands clasped, resting on the space between us, until he pulled over when we reached the outer limits of Locust Grove.

"Remember when life was much simpler?" He turned off the ignition and turned himself in the seat to face me. Taking both my hands in his, he put them up to his lips and gently kissed each one. "No."

"No, what?" I couldn't help but get lost in his deep blue eyes.

"Earlier you asked me if I was here to arrest you; I'm not. I gave it up." Looking down, he shook his head. "I wasn't going to leave you in this time of need so the Order of Elders made me choose."

My mouth dropped. He smiled.

"I told them I wanted to give up all my spiritual powers." He dropped his head. Reaching over, I pulled his chin up so I could get an intuition reading off his body language. If the eyes are truly the path to someone's soul, I should be able to see his with no problem. And since he was no longer a spiritualist, I can read him as much as I want to without his permission. "What?"

Closing my eyes, I inhaled, and then inhaled again. . .only deeper.

"What? Why did you inhale twice?" His voice drifted into a hushed whisper.

Slowly, I opened my eyes and a smile crossed my lips. "The first time I was reading your intuition." My heart fluttered. "The second was because you smell so good."

"Awww...my little witch." He slid over and wrapped me in his arms. Kissing the top of my forehead, he assured me, "We are going to figure this out, but I'm afraid I'm not going to be of any help."

"Of course you are." Just because he wasn't a spiritualist didn't mean he wasn't a good cop. "You were a police officer before we knew about our spiritual gifts and you will continue to use those skills now."

"You know what?" there was eagerness in his eyes. "You're right! I *was* good."

"You *are* good!" I confirmed, twisting in my seat to face him. I grabbed the sides of his face and kissed him. "Now, let's get back to figuring out who killed Kenny."

As much as I wanted to reminisce about the past, I didn't have a lot of time to figure out who was trying to frame me from not only Kenny's murder, but also the stolen ostrich and June's Gems. Things were progressing fast in the spiritual world. With the banning of me living in the village and the Order of the Elders sent, I didn't need my intuition to tell me that the evidence had built up against me.

"Let's start with the facts." Leaning over me, Oscar opened the glove box and searched through it.

"What are you looking for?" I questioned as he pulled out a napkin.

"Paper. Don't you have any scrap paper in here?"

"Where is your little pad?" I noticed he didn't have his usual cop stuff out, including that annoying notebook he writes in.

"They took it." He found a chewed up pen in the there as well. "They took everything."

"This is a good thing." I had to find a light in the tunnel. "Besides, you never really learned how to use your sorcery powers or even went to school."

"I was never very comfortable with the whole idea. I like old school investigations." He held the pen and napkin up in the air, and then slid back over to the driver's seat. "Let's get started. There isn't much time."

Oscar reconfirmed my fear…not much time.

It was just like old times, watching him take notes as I answered all his questions about where I was when all the incidents took place.

And then came the explosive question.

"Why in the world would you ask all over Whispering Falls how to get in touch with Kenny?" He waited. I bit the corner of my lip, wondering if I should just come clean about Belur.

There wasn't a reason I shouldn't tell him now. He wasn't the sheriff in charge. He was just my boyfriend trying to help me out.

"Have you ever seen the show I Dream of Jeannie?" I put my hands together and placed them over my head like a genie and bobbled my head side-to-side. He nodded. "Well, I think Kenny accidentally left a genie in the sage pile he left at A Charming Cure because I'm now the master of Belur, a big purple genie. Turban, pointy shoes, bottle and all."

"Why is that a problem?"

My eyes narrowed. There was something going on within Oscar's body that I wasn't able to pinpoint.

"Who wouldn't want a genie?" He tapped the pen to his temple. "I'd love to have him. Wish to find the killer."

"I can't wish a wish like that. It's against all the spiritual rules and I'd hate to see what they'd do to me." I shudder at the possibilities.

"What who would do to you?" Oscar asked. He was all sorts of confused.

"The spiritual community." I laughed. This decision of leaving his powers had to be affecting him more than he wanted to admit.

"June, don't tell me you believe in all the witchcraft, voodoo crap." Vigorously he wrote on the napkin and then pointed to the word 'genie'. "You really believe that you believe in genies now." He scoffed. "Let me guess. . ." he rubbed his chin, "...big guy in Tone Loc pants?"

"We do live in Whispering Falls." I reminded him. "And yes, a genie."

"You do, but I live in Locust Grove." He put the pen and paper in his lap and looked at me. He was serious. "Where I have always lived. You went to Whispering Falls to open the shop. Are you sure you can, for sure, one hundred percent, say you didn't kill that guy? You might be sniffing too much of those herbs you call cures."

"I...I..." Suddenly, I realized that without his spiritual gift, Oscar had no recollection of the past year and a half. It was as if he was slipping back into the Oscar Park I knew before we moved to Whispering Falls. The pre-spiritualist Oscar Park. "Of course I didn't kill him and that is why I came to you. I need your help."

"And you have it." He put the Green Machine in drive and headed into Locust Grove. "I've got to get to work. The chief is going to kill me for being late."

Oscar talked on and on about the new projects Locust Grove police station was doing and told all of these stories as if he had never left. If this was the case, did he not know that I was a spiritualist, a witch of sorts?

"Thanks for breakfast." He put the car in park right in front of his childhood home, across the street from Darla's and my old house. "Spending time with my best friend is a great way to start the day. Especially, since you barely have time for me since you moved and work all day."

Breakfast? Best Friend? His memory of the past was being replaced right in front of my eyes.

"Yea, you're welcome." I slid over to the driver's side when he got out. My heart sunk to my tippy toes.

"I'll call you later this afternoon so we can work on this little murder thing." He gave me a strange look before he slammed the car door. "Try not to worry."

I watched him walk into the house.

Rowr, rowr. Mr. Prince Charming jumped down from the dashboard and planted his paws on the windowsill, looking at the house.

Just a few days ago when I had gone into Locust Grove to go to the Piggly Wiggly, I had passed our old houses. Both of them looked run down and unkept. Today they are vibrant and welcoming.

"So I guess Oscar's memory of being a spiritualist was wiped out when he decided he didn't want to leave me and our. . ." A lump settled in my throat. Tears welled in my eyes, "he doesn't remember our relationship?"

Meow, meow. Mr. Prince Charming sat down on the passenger side, dragging his tail along the seat.

"I will get him back." I vowed before putting the Green Machine in drive and heading into Locust Grove.

Chapter Seventeen

The Piggly Wiggly parking lot was full of cars, which really shouldn't be a surprise since it was the only grocery store within twenty miles of Locust Grove.

"Ugh!" I sighed when there weren't any spots near the front of the store, and parked in the last spot way in the back of the lot. "Okay, Madame Torres." I pulled her out of my bag. Resisting the urge to ask her about Oscar, I asked to see Adeline. The ball glowed green with black electric lines like a spider's web. The glow dampened to a pale yellow as Adeline's office inside the Piggly Wiggly came into focus.

She was sitting at her desk shaking her fist at the same person I had seen in my crystal ball before. By the look in her eyes, I could tell she wasn't happy and they were arguing. I had to get in there and see who he was.

I couldn't help but think he was part of the missing June's Gems that I was sure Adeline had stolen in order to keep George. She would do anything to keep him and she has proven that over and over by coming to A Charming

Cure for potions dealing with love, or at least that was what my intuition told me.

"Oh, no!" I held Madame Torres inches from my face. "Is all of this my fate since I used a love potion on Adeline?"

"Yes!" A puff of smoke gave way to Mary Ellen, the younger of the three elders, who was sitting cross legged in the passenger seat with Mr. Prince Charming in her lap.

Purr, purr. He was happily curled up.

"I've always adored you, Mr. Prince Charming." She continued to scratch his ears. "Yes, you are in a tad bit of trouble."

"And you appear just like that?" I waved my hands in the air.

"Of course." She smiled, her eyes narrowing. "We are a lot alike. I was a village president at one time as well as young and fun and got in trouble a time or two."

"I didn't do anything they are accusing me of." I tried to get an intuition reading from her. "We are nothing alike. I wish I had the cool powers you had, plus your fashion sense."

She had exchanged the leopard print coat for a long red form-fitting cloak that showed off her curves perfectly. Her long black hair, which was straight when I first met her, lay in loose curls across her shoulders.

"We have a lot more in common than you think. You will find out soon enough." She picked up Madame Torres and tapped the ball. True to form, Madame Torres didn't appear. She didn't like too many people other than me. "She's a wicked one."

"She is." Carefully I took Madame Torres from her. The last thing I needed today was a mad ball.

"Anyway," she brushed her hands together as if Madame Torres made her dirty, "you had distinct orders not to perform spells on any other spiritualist, which you went ahead and did with Faith." Her eyes darkened. "Not to mention the little love stuff you are helping Adeline with." She pointed toward the Piggly Wiggly.

"I guess you do know all that I have done." I hung my head in shame. The edges of my hair tickled my chin, making me want long hair like Mary Ellen's.

"We all do. I'm the only one willing to help you."

Just as quickly as she appeared, she disappeared, only this time the smoke was hot pink.

"Just like you to leave in style!" I shouted out into the air.

Mary Ellen's cackle echoed in the Green Machine, making me laugh. I had to assume she would show up when she had something to tell me or let me know how she was going to help me. I wasn't holding my breath.

"I'll be right back," I assured Mr. Prince Charming. Surely if he thought I was in danger he would have tried to stop me, but he didn't.

The Piggly Wiggly was busy and I was happy I wasn't grocery shopping. Taking a detour down aisle five, just in case there happened to be any Ding Dongs, I made my way back to the office. I only hoped I wasn't too late to see who she was talking to.

Putting my ear to the door, I listened. I didn't hear anything. I tapped on the door and heard footsteps.

"June?" Adeline questioned. "What are you doing here?" She held the door tight to her body. The crack was too small for me to see in the room, but I rolled up on my tippy toes to peer in just in case.

Nothing.

"I wanted to ask you about yoga." I rolled up and down on my toes again. "I'm sure this is some sort of yoga move."

I did my best to cover up my strange behavior.

"Sure, come on in." She opened the door revealing she was the only one in the room. "There really aren't a lot of options out there. I have been looking."

She plopped down on the ground. Her legs outstretched in front of her. She bent one leg, placing her heel under the opposite thigh, and repeating the same move with her other leg, crossing them. She positioned herself with her spine, neck and body erect. I wondered what she was doing as she placed her hands on her knees, with her palms up.

"Ohoomm. . ." she moaned with her eyes closed. "This is Sukasana pose. It helps clear a busy mind and creates inner harmony."

Inner harmony?

"Is your harmony off?" I questioned. "I can give you a ...er...remedy for that." I tried to tap into her intuition, but was drawing a blank.

Her eyes popped open, "Not that I don't think your remedies work, but George is right. I can't rely on you for all of my quirks."

"Why not?" My nose got a whiff of chocolate. Throwing my head in the air, I took another sniff as my intuition led me near Adeline's desk. The scent was stronger and my gut pulled. I had no idea what I was looking for and had to keep questioning her to find whatever it was. "They aren't necessarily remedies. They just sort of help you cope."

She was busy looking for inner harmony with her eyes closed and she didn't notice me searching around.

"You are kind of my go-to pal for all things I have problems with. So maybe we should do more things as friends."

My eyes widened and my stomach churned when I saw the half-eaten June's Gem in the trash can. How did she get it? When did she get it? More importantly, why on earth would she not finish it?

"June?" Suddenly she was standing next to me.

"Uh. Huh?" Startled, I jumped around, trying to figure out what was going on. My mind was cloudy.

"I said we should do more things as friends instead of the therapist type of relationship we having going on." She put her hand on her desk and leaned on it. "Like yoga. It seems like we could both use a little stress relief."

Keep your friends close, but your enemies closer. Darla's tried-and-true words to live by rang in my head. Sometimes Darla's little quotes came in handy, but I didn't always agree on her natural way of living, especially with food.

I looked up as if Darla could see me, and wondered what she was thinking about the whole Ding Dong situation. I couldn't help but think that she was happy. She hated the chocolatey goodies.

"June?" Adeline's eyebrows rose as she put her face inches from mine. "See, you aren't really here. You are out in la-la land." She poked my shoulder. "That is why you need yoga."

"Well, I did come here to ask about it."

"Great!" She jumped in place. "I can come to your house or you can come to mine." She scribbled her address on a piece of paper and handed it to me. "We can try a few things I found on the internet until we find a yoga studio."

"How about your place?"

Her place was perfect! I would be able to snoop around to see if she had anything to do with the June's Gems missing from Wicked Good. The more I thought about how she could steal from Raven and pin it on me the madder I got.

"Sure." She smiled, rounding her cheeks into rosy mounds. "Call before you come."

"I will do that." I rolled my eyes at her, but she didn't see it. She was too busy looking at her watch.

"Hey, I will be right back." Hurriedly she walked to the door. "I have a very important delivery today and I want to see if it's here yet.

"Important delivery?" I spat the words out contemptuously after she left the room. Looking down at the trash can, I couldn't help but get angrier and angrier trying to figure why she would do such a thing. "What are you up too, Adeline?" I pumped my fist to the side, just as a puff of smoke filled the air around me.

"What the…" I blinked several times as I realized my hands were gripping the steering wheel of the Green

Machine. Quickly I let go as if I were touching fire. ". . .hell!"

My breath caught in my throat as my heart pounded.

Meow, meow. Mr. Prince Charming sat ever so elegantly on the passenger seat with a smug little smile on his face. If only he could talk.

"Madame Torres." I grabbed her out of my bag and held her up to my face. "What was that?"

"What?" She yawned.

"I'm sorry; did I wake you up from your little nap?" I sarcastically added, not letting her answer. "How in the world did I go from inside of Adeline's office to here without walking out of there?" I pointed to the front of the store with one hand and held her up to see with the other.

"I don't know. Maybe it's some sort of new gift you got since you took over as village president." She did worry about my little mishap too much as she brought her fingernails up to her eyes to inspect them. "Maybe you need to ask *the elders.* They seem to be know-it-alls."

"I'm serious. Do you know anything about this?" I held her up to my face. This was not a normal gift for me.

"I am an intuitionist, not a. . .well. . . *witch.* " The word left my mouth in a hushed whisper.

Placing my hand over my opened mouth that I couldn't seem to shut, my mind started drifting with all sorts of possibilities. These were thoughts that would have never crossed my mind. When I accepted the position, did it really come with all sorts of powers that I had never even dreamed of? Did all my powers have to match or even go beyond those of the citizens in the community?

Blankly, I stared out the windshield. I wasn't sure what to do. Oscar's memory had been swiped clean as if he never knew he was a spiritualist, and he obviously had no clue I was one, so he was not someone I could talk to.

Eloise thinks I'm on house arrest and when she finds out I left, she will be mad.

The Elders won't help me; they are only worried about 'making sure the community doesn't get a bad name.'

Hiss, hiss. Mr. Prince Charming's back raised up as if he knew exactly what I was thinking.

"I hate to, but it's my only hope." I rubbed down his back, thinking about Aunt Helena and vividly picturing

Hidden Hall, A Spiritualist University before I plunged my hands down to my side.

Chapter Eighteen

That wasn't so bad, I thought as I looked down the street of the University. I could probably get use to traveling around this way.

Mr. Prince Charming darted ahead of me. He knew his way around and would be fine.

"Nice to see you," the voice came before I saw the body.

"Hi, Gus." I would recognize his voice from anywhere. "It's lovely to hear you."

"And to see you." His mischievous smile appeared before his tall lanky body did.

Gus was a shape-shifting Clairvoyant. He was all over the place and reading the dead better than anyone I had ever know. Well. . .I guess I didn't know many, but he was good at it.

"You got your hair cut." I said.

There was a sense of more of a grown-up Gus from the last time I had seen him.

He brushed his hands through the shorter version of his old shaggy ash-blond hair. His brown eyes rolled, "Your aunt told me I needed to be more presentable if I was going to continue to be her assistant."

"Well, you certainly are trying." I noticed his usual cargo shorts and T-shirt had been replace by khaki pants and a button-down, though his sleeves were rolled up to his elbows.

"Are you here to finish your classes?" he asked as we walked toward campus.

The streets were filled with students. Many more than I recall being there before.

"I'm working on my level twenty-eight and a few other things." I didn't want to tell him everything. "What's with all the students?"

"Since you left, the University opened up the divide between the Dark-Siders and Good-Siders."

"Oh." My eyebrows lifted in delight as I looked down the street toward the edge of the University where the Dark-Siders lived, and I noticed it had become a much brighter area.

The Dark-Siders and Good-Siders could never really get along well enough to co-habit. Luckily, I was able to show them we could live in harmony the last time I was here. It was hard, and both sides still have to refrain from using their gifts on the other, but it seemed to be working out pretty well.

"Yea." He nodded toward the edge of town. "Even the wooded area has gotten a lot sunnier."

"That's great." I laughed, recalling the time I had snuck over to Raven Mortimer's to spy on her when I was a student. She is a Dark-Sider and her sister is a Good-Sider.

That was taboo back in the day, but this was a new day and everyone needed to get along, good or bad.

"You did a good thing here." He swept his hands in front of him like the models on the Price Is Right game show. "Enrollment is up. Morale is up. Everyone is happy, including your Aunt."

"I hope she's in a good mood today." I winked.

Aunt Helena had always been a hard nut to crack, so anytime I could find her in a good mood in my favor, the better. She was my only hope.

"There is something different about you, June Heal." Gus stopped and rubbed his chin. He stared at me. I looked away. I didn't want him to see into my soul.

"I'm not sure what you are talking about." I said looking up, but he was gone.

Without hesitation, I made my way down past the library where the administration offices were. Aunt Helena's office was there, but she rarely was. A lot of the time, she was substituting for a class. She believed it kept her in tune with the students, when the students would have rather stayed in bed if the teacher was absent.

The sun was always the brightest over the library. It was a great place for all the spiritualists to learn harmony. After all, the books in there told everyone everything they needed to know about each other and their gifts.

"Hello." I nodded and smiled as I passed the students running up the library stairs.

I never saw myself as the college type since I didn't have the opportunity to go to college since Darla died, but after being here and taking classes, I did enjoy it.

Mewl, mewl. Mr. Prince Charming was sitting next to old Elory, the dog that lived in Whispering Falls.

I couldn't help but smile. Anywhere else, it would be strange to see a pristine white cat sitting next to a dog that wore a long scarf that covered his head and wearing a couple of strands of pearls around his neck. But not here. It had become the normal way of life for me.

My mind drifted back to Oscar. My gut told me things were going to be rocky for us. If there even *was* an 'us'.

"June!" Aunt Helena was walking out the door of the administration building. "I was expecting you, but not so quickly."

She wrapped her arms around me, and guided me back toward the campus. The students suddenly stirred clear of our path, not making eye contact with my Aunt or me.

"I'm assuming you are figuring out all the new *gifts* you are getting." There was pride in her voice.

"I don't really know of any but the whole disappearing thing." I fluttered my hands in the air. "The smoke I could do away with."

"Smoke?" She stopped in the wheat field just shy of the sign with several long wooden arms, each with a finger pointing in a different direction. Each wooden arm had a different school on it.

"Yes, the whole teleportation thing that you do." Looking at her, something clicked in my mind. She had no idea what I was talking about. A more terrifying realization swept over me. If she didn't know what was going on with me, who did?

Without a word, she tapped the sign toward Potion School. Then magically, a pathway appeared across the wheat field.

My eyes followed as the path gained momentum and ended at a small pink cottage that had window boxes under each window overflowing with Geraniums, Morning Glories, Petunias, Moon Flowers and Trailing Ivy, leaving a rainbow of colorful explosion.

Unable to enjoy all of the lovely flowers, I hurried alongside of her. Her long cloak flapped behind her, creating a very eerie sound.

"Aunt Helena?" I questioned with fear in my voice. She knew something and was not telling me what it was.

"It can't be." She hurried into the cottage where there were a handful of students silently waiting for class to begin. A hushed gasp came from them.

"Yes, yes." Aunt Helena tapped the cauldron on the table without looking up. The cauldron started to bubble before she even put anything in it. The foam rose just shy of the top so not to spill over. "This is June, my niece." She turned toward me. "Everyone knows who you are. Especially since you took over as Whispering Falls Village President."

I didn't know whether that was good or bad, until I saw the latest issue of UnHidden Hall, the University newspaper, or should I say smut rag?

The headlines read: *Former Hidden Hall Prodigy On House Arrest!*

There was a picture of me doing a smudging ceremony to accompany it.

"I…" I grabbed the paper and quickly read through, fully aware that all eyes were on me, including Aunt Helena's. Nervously, I laughed and held my wrists out in front of me.

I need my bracelet. If there were ever a time I could use some good luck and protection, it would be nice if it were now. I didn't want to risk anyone turning me in if they knew they could get a price for it. "I'm obviously not on house arrest. See?" I shoved my wrists in the air. "It's all a misunderstanding." I smiled, making sure I looked each of them in the eye. I wanted to see if I could tap into my intuition to see if any of them were going to rat me out.

All I smelled was fear. Good.

Aunt Helena cleared her throat. "Now that that is out of the way we can start our lesson on level twenty-eight." She drew her long pointy finger out in front of her. "June, you can sit there."

Before taking my little stool at the front table, I noticed that everyone in the class was much different from the classes I had taken before.

"What? I guess you think all witches have warts and pointy hats?" A plump girl snarled making the freckles on the bridge of her nose come together forming the shape of a bat.

"Um. . .witch?" I jerked around looking at all the students, and then to Aunt Helena.

"Yes, June." She put her hands together, bringing them down to her waist. "A level twenty-eight is potions using witchcraft. They are very tricky spells and only the village president's can know them outside of the witchery world."

I listened intently as Aunt Helena explained the first stages of level twenty-eight, but I believe it was for my benefit since all the other students groaned and rolled their eyes as she continued to talk.

To me it was fascinating to hear about different hexes and spells that I would have never dreamed existed. The possibilities were endless in the ways I could help customers, and more importantly, Oscar.

There had to be a way of helping him get some part of his memory back. Hopefully, the most important part he would remember would be *me*.

"I want everyone to work on a *return hex* for homework." Aunt Helena walked around the room giving details of what she wanted from them. A collective groan filled the room.

I don't even know what a return hex is. I flipped through the manual that was sitting in front of me, trying to figure out this mumbo-jumbo.

"Really? Because you have got some really bad ju-ju following you around." The plump girl eyed me up and down. "Which means someone has put a bad hex on you."

My brows furrowed. I didn't realize I had said that out loud.

"You didn't say it out loud. I can read your mind." She tapped her temple, leaving a small indent in the fleshy skin. "Bad hex."

"Bad hex?" Fear knotted inside my gut as my intuition lit fire. Never in a million years did I believe someone would put an evil spell on me.

Was this the reason for the murder? The break-in at Wicked Good? Or worse, why was someone framing me?

I tried to concentrate on all the things Aunt Helena was teaching, but my mind continued to go back to the last couple of days and the realization that I've got to do whatever I can to figure this mess out.

"June?" Aunt Helena tapped the edge of my tabletop. "Class is dismissed."

I looked around at the empty tables behind me. I was so consumed with my thoughts that I didn't know everyone had left.

"I'm assuming you aren't staying." Aunt Helena sat down on the empty stool next to me. Her cloak swished around her. She put her hand on my knee.

I nodded. "I have to get back to Eloise's and try to stay out of trouble while I figure all of this out."

"Though I'd love for you to stay here, I know you are bull-headed and won't. My only advice is to rely on your stable gift of intuition to guide you. The level-twenty eight talents will come when you need them. You must stay safe. Be a good girl and play by their rules." There was some caution in her voice. "You will figure this out."

"I hope so." I glanced out of the window at the passing students wearing smiles on their faces, without a care in the world.

There was no time to waste. I gathered up my bag and gave Aunt Helena a quick hug.

Mr. Prince Charming was waiting on the steps when I walked out.

Mewl, mewl. He batted at a spiderweb that was wrapped between the spindles on the steps.

"No time to dilly-dally." I shook my finger at him.. "We've got to go figure this thing out."

I picked up Mr. Prince Charming and held him close to my body. If I was going to do this teletransporting, I didn't want to do it without him.

I envisioned us sitting on the couch in Eloise's tree house before I plunged my free fist the ground.

Chapter Nineteen

"I'm not about to ask where you have been," Eloise called out from the deck of the tree house. "But if you do it again, I won't be able to cover for you."

"Why didn't you tell me about Oscar?" I asked. Finding out what happened to him and our life together was more important to me than being framed for murder or thievery.

"I had no idea that most things happen until after they happen." Eloise walked into the house and held her hand out. "Brunch is waiting."

Eloise had the best gardens in any spiritual community around. Lanterns hung from the trees dotted the gravel pathway with beautiful flowers planted on both sides. I ran my hand along the vibrant purple, green, red, orange and yellow flowers. Wisteria vines provided a fragrant canopy leading to a clearing.

There were rows and rows of herbs, neatly planted and perfectly proportioned on the way to the gazebo where Eloise had brunch ready. Mr. Prince Charming's tail waved above the rows as he darted in and out of the herbs ahead of us.

Each row had a painted wooden sign with the names of the herbs that followed in line. Herbs I had never heard of. I walked in front of each row, touching each herb sign.

"Rose petals, moonflower, mandrake root, seaweed, shrinking violet, dream dust, fairy dust, magic peanut, lucky clover, steal rose," I whispered, remembering the simpler times I had spent here.

The mismatched tea setting was perfect for the occasion. Everything was mismatched these days. Quickly I counted five chairs, five china cups, five saucers, and a large assortment of pastries from Wicked Good.

"Are we expecting company?" I was in no mood for chitchat with anyone.

"You will be seeing a lot of us, dearie," Mary Lynn floated above the table. She stretched out her gloved hand, reaching out to grab a scone.

"Stop that!" Mary Sue appeared next to Mary Lynn and smacked Mary Lynn's hand away. "That's rude."

"Don't tell *us* what's rude!" Mary Ellen appeared next to the table in a hot pink tutu and wearing a tiara nestled in her black hair. "You are the queen of rude in how you treat people."

"I knew the day you were chosen that it was a mistake." Mary Sue and Mary Lynn took their seats at the table.

"Can't we all get along?" Mary Lynn adjusted her fox stole and picked at her curls.

"Well it was." Mary Sue wasn't going to let any of the younger elders tell her what was what. "She is entirely too young to be an elder and *she* is entirely too young to be a Village president." She pointed her sharp nail toward me.

"Leave me out of this." I pulled a seat out and sat down. The faster we got this over with the better. Eloise rolled her eyes and started to fill the teacups with delicious dark tea.

"This looks good." Mary Ellen leaned over her cup and took a whiff of the steam. "Naughty, naughty." Mary Ellen waved a finger in Eloise's direction. "Trying to disguise different herbs to achieve harmony." Mary Ellen referred to the tea. She knew Eloise was trying to keep the peace.

"What? Blackberry is for healing. We need the healing." Eloise made sure she had the perfect combination for all of her guests. "Now, let's all get along and figure out how to get June out of this mess and my nephew back to where he belongs."

"Oh my." Mary Lynn grabbed the napkin and lifted it to her mouth as she shook her head.

"He will never be back the way he was." Mary Sue reached over and patted Mary Lynn's hand.

"What do you mean?" A spark shot from Eloise's finger when she point toward the unfriendly Mary.

Mary Ellen jumped up and stood between a sitting Mary Sue and a standing Eloise. "Like you said, we all need to get along." Mary Ellen put her hands out as Eloise came closer. "You know what happens when someone denounces their powers."

"He only denounced it until the crimes are solved." Eloise glared back and forth between the Mary's. If looks could kill, there would be three more murders on my hands.

"You only have one time to denounce your powers, and that is forever." Mary Sue snapped her fingers. A book appeared in her hand. She placed it on the table and used her finger in the air to flip the pages. When it stopped, she pointed to a page. "Right here."

Eloise leaned in closer. With her eyes squinted she let out a loud gasp. Slowly, she turned toward me. Her eyes were set back in her head, dark circles quickly forming around them.

"No, no, no." I stood up, knocking the chair on the floor. "No! I did not sign up for this!"

"Whether you signed on the dotted line or not, this is your life." Mary Sue jabbed at the page. "He was told the consequences of what would happen if he denounced his powers in order to come back here and help you."

"Yes, he erased of all his spiritual memories and of even living here." Mary Lynn twisted her hand in the air and Oscar appeared in a cloud of gray smoke.

"I have to help her! I don't care if you erase my memory and I don't remember being a spiritualist. I love her and love conquers all. We will come back together because we are destined to be together."

My heart broke watching the conversation he had before the Marys had stripped him of his powers.

"I have to go back and help her. She needs me. Take away all of my spiritual gifts and memory!"

"No!" I screamed, reaching out to the gray cloud right before it disappeared into mid-air. I scurried over to Eloise who was bent over clutching her stomach. She and Oscar had just found each other after years of her searching for him after his evil uncle had kidnapped him. "I'm so sorry. I'm so sorry."

She pushed me away and scrambled to her feet. In silence, I watched as she ran back down the cobblestone walk toward the tree house.

"Look what you have done!" I scolded the Marys. "After everything she has done for you. You should be ashamed."

"She asked." Mary Sue shrugged. "We aren't in the business of sugar-coating things. We are in the business of fixing the spiritual world when our *leaders* screw up."

"And you couldn't talk him out of it?" I walked around the table, glaring at each one of them. Mary Lynn's eyes were filled with tears and Mary Ellen wouldn't even look at me. Mary Sue was the one who was responsible.

The sky filled with dark clouds and a clap of thunder was loud and clear followed up by a vicious bolt of lightning.

"Time to go." Mary Lynn put her thumb and finger together as if she was going to snap her way out.

I grabbed her hands. "Time to go where?"

"The funeral." Mary Ellen twirled her finger in the air instantly changing her outfit into a black tight mini-dress and a large brimmed floppy hat.

Kenny.

Chapter Twenty

I didn't go back in the house to see if Eloise was okay. I knew she needed space and I needed to give it to her. After all, it was because of me that Oscar gave up his spiritual life. But he was right. We would come back together because we were destined to be together.

"Forever," I whispered as I stood on the edge of the forest and Whispering Falls. I closed my eyes and concentrated on a disguise. "I wish to be disguised so I can go to Kenny's funeral and not be recognized."

When I opened my eyes, I was standing at the bottom of the steps of Two Sisters and A Funeral, covered in head-to-toe pink. Even my bag had been turned pink. Everything, all the way down to hot pink eye shadow and blush. I looked like someone had taken me to the Pepto Bismal factory and dipped me into the vat.

"A Fairy?" I murmured. I had no idea how these powers worked, and I liked them, but I'm far from a pink fairy girl. "Fine." I waved the wand in the air and ran up the steps, stopping shy of the door. "Excuse me." I looked behind me and realized I had seen my image in the funeral home's doors and thought someone was behind me.

I rotated from left to right and took a good look.

Hiss, hiss. Mr. Prince Charming was very vocal about his distaste of the wings and tiara.

"And you think I like it?" I scowled. "You stay here."

What good would my fairy disguise be if Mr. Prince Charming tagged along? Cautiously, I opened the door. The foyer and steps were packed. All sorts of spiritualists were there, including some of Kenny's tribesmen, or at least they looked like and dressed like him.

No one paid any attention to me as I stood there.

"There is no way she's going to show up here." A familiar voice walked up in line behind me.

Fluttering my wings, I slightly turned around to see who Petunia was talking to. I recognized her voice and I wondered who she was talking about.

"I heard she was put on house arrest." Faith stood next to Petunia with Raven on the other side.

"I haven't heard anything from the winds." Faith's eyes grew big and she lowered her voice, "But I wouldn't put it past her to have killed him. She was probably mad he wasn't doing his spiritual job right."

Petunia's hazel eyes blinked rapidly, followed by an open stare. I watched her closely. After all, she was still on my list of suspects.

Great, the two of them together were bashing me when both of them are mad at me. I refrained from turning around and giving them a piece of my mind. My heart pounded in the confines of my pink tutu as my mind raced. One of them had to be the killer. Each of them threatened me on the day of Kenny's death.

I had to get to Oscar and give him all the information I had, even if he didn't have spiritual powers, he was still my best friend.

"Do they know anything about the break-in at your bakery?" Petunia was baiting Raven.

Raven was tight-lipped and she shook her head no. Why wasn't she standing up for me? She was mad at Kenny too for not making his deliveries on time.

"Probably June." Faith held her chin up with her nostrils flaring. "She was always bugging Raven to make her some."

Liar! My wings were flapping so hard, I thought they were going to lift me off the ground. It took everything I had in me not to use the pink wand and turn her into a wretched toad. Why was Faith doing this? Slowly I turned around.

The three of them turned to the front, coming face-to-face with me.

"I love your wings." Faith smiled, scrunching her nose. "Pink is my favorite color," she squealed and drew her shoulders up toward her ears.

I waved my wand in the air, making sure I didn't open my mouth. None of them recognized me. Raven stared, sending a cold chill to the tips of my Fairy wings. For a brief moment, our eyes locked. I looked away, just in case she did see something in my soul.

"Why couldn't we have cool fairy wings?" Faith had Fairy envy. I could feel her onyx eyes giving my wings the once-over. I made sure to do a little extra flutter with each step as the line moved forward.

"Stop staring." Raven told Faith, and then turned her attention to Petunia. "Has the ostrich returned?"

"Not a feather. I wish someone would take that talking bird." She crossed her arms. "It talks so much I have a hard time hearing myself think."

"Again...June." Faith said. I wasn't sure, but I think there was some pleasure in her voice as she accused me of everything. "I heard she wanted one of those feathers for some sort of spell. And I told Officer Gandalf all of this. She thinks she's invincible, being the village president and all, but she has another thing coming to her. She's not invincible. She got caught this time."

"Who is Officer Gandalf?" Raven's nose scrunched up.

"I have no idea." Faith shrugged. "He was in the Tea Shoppe and said he was here to help in the investigations, so I told him what I knew."

She told that nosey officer? Turning away, I covered my mouth. I couldn't believe she was pinning all of this on me. What happened to loyalty? I just saved her life a few months ago. Did she suddenly forget about that?

I lifted my wand in the air. I was going to give her a little jolt, but out of the corner of my eye I could see Mac and Gandalf, the new sheriff, in a heated discussion. Mac's face had turned all sorts of shades as he pushed his chest out in protest to whatever it was Gandalf was saying.

Faith wasn't worth a real accident being pinned on me, so I eased my way over to the corner where Mac and Gandolf stood in line so I could hear whatever they were saying for myself. I had a sneaky suspicion the heated argument was about my case.

"Mac, you know as well as I do all the evidence points to your client." Gandalf placed his hand on his baton and stood firm.

"Like what?" Mac pushed his glasses up on his nose. He might come to Gandalf's chest, but he was a mighty little man. "Just because a cupcake was named after her doesn't mean she broke into Wicked Good. Just because she tried to help her friend catch a runaway animal doesn't mean she took the animal, and the search of her property proved it. Just because she needed new smudging ingredients for the ceremony and she needed to get in touch with Kenny doesn't mean she killed him."

"Her hand is dipped into every single piece of the pie." Gandalf huffed.

"There is no council that will convict her based on the evidence you think you have." Mac shot back.

Mac was doing a fine job standing up for me. I admit we had our differences when he was my neighbor when I lived in Locust Grove. Little did I know he was actually living there by order of Izzy to keep watch over Darla and me after we moved away from Whispering Falls when my father died.

"I'm going to make sure they do." Gandolf tugged on his sagging pants, pulling them up. "I have some eye witnesses that say she was at odds with all sorts of community members. I've seen where being named village president and having that power can go to their heads. This just might be the case."

Hrumph. Mac cleared his throat and moved ahead with the line.

Don't believe him Mac. That darn Faith.

I continued to walk around to see if I heard anything that would give me a clue, but everyone was as tight-lipped as Kenny was up front in that coffin.

The Karimas did a good job on him. He was head-to-toe in original Native American dress.

I fluttered by, bowing my head in respect and took a seat in the back of the large room where the service was being held. It was the only seat available and there was still a line out the door.

Everyone was there paying their respects. Izzy was up front in the far right corner, which seemed to be where the Karimas had seated the family. I wasn't sure, but it looked like Kenny was married. Her face was barely visible under her black veil, but her long brown hair fell braided down her back. A young man seated next to her looked exactly like a younger version of Kenny.

My heart broke for them.

"I really like your wings." A breath hit the back of my neck. "Yes, I like them."

Startled, I jumped around to find Patience Karima reaching her fat little finger out to touch my fluttering gems.

"Very sparkly." She reached farther and her eyes twinkled. "Very sparkly."

Before she could touch me, I got up and walked to the standing-room-only crowd, leaving a very disappointed looked on her face. I knew she meant no harm; she never did, but who likes their space invaded? Or their wings touched?

Between the ceremonial music and chants, the service was long and my legs were getting sweaty from standing in these tights. I excused myself and moved out into the hallway. I wanted to be sure I stayed until the end of the service and make it down for the reception. People tend to talk more freely when they are eating, and not to mention I'm starving since I didn't get to eat a pastry at Eloise's tea that was a bust.

After a few minutes of gathering my thoughts, I was about to return when someone slipped out the side door. The profile caught the corner of my eye.

"What the. . ." I watched the person carefully shut the door behind them before I rushed over to take a peek. The long trench coat and large dark sunglasses would have been a great cover-up if Adeline had worn a wig to go with it. Her short blonde hair was a dead giveaway though.

I ducked back into the door when she turned around to get one last look at the funeral home from the bottom of the steps. I peeled back the curtains from the window to get a better look and make sure it was Adeline. It was confirmed when she took off her glasses and wiped her eyes.

"Returning to the scene of the crime are you?" I whispered and drummed my fingers together.

Why? I wondered as I watched her run down the street. What would be her reasoning to kill Kenny?

My pink bag glowed a hot pink. Looking around, I made sure no one was out in the hallway before I started to check all the closed doors to see if any were unlocked. I couldn't trust Madame Torres to be quiet and I couldn't risk being caught by anyone from the community. Especially dressed as a fairy.

The second door I tried was unlocked. Without making a sound, I closed the door behind me and didn't worry with flipping on a light. I didn't want to see any dead people, or even know what was in the room. Everything I saw Patience doing the other day gave me the heebie-jeebies.

Madame Torres appeared. She wasn't in her usual colors of reds, purples, and greens.

"Did you do this in honor of me?" I asked about her appearance in all pink.

"Shhh…." She held a finger to her hot pink lips, and her eyes bulged, filling the entire glass ball. Madame Torres let a firework display burst out before the ball went black.

"You wanted me to see fireworks?" I didn't understand this at all.

"Shhhh!" And then Adeline appeared as she had a couple of days ago at the shop.

"I knew you'd know what to do. I swear you are way better than my doctor." Madame Torres replayed the words Adeline had spoken.

"You really should go to your doctor." I encouraged her. *"I'm not a doctor. I just know how to put herbs together."*

It was surreal to watch myself having a conversation from a few days ago. I had forgotten that Adeline wanted Belur's bottle and really didn't like what I had to say.

"What was that?" I asked Madame Torres when something Adeline was doing struck me funny.

The scene rewound like a tape and Madame Torres played it back in slow motion. During the conversation, I had walked around trying to figure out why I couldn't read

Adeline, but Adeline was mocking me behind my back when I told her she didn't need a remedy.

"Madame Torres," I gasped, "Do you think she was seeking revenge because I wouldn't give her a remedy the other day?"

The ball went black, just like the room.

"Madame Torres?" There was noise coming from out in the hallway. I didn't know whether Madame Torres shut off because someone might see her glow from under the door, or if I was right and Adeline was seeking revenge.

"Ouch!" I thrust my fists to my side and Teletransported by accident, ending up in Eloise's garden next to the aloe.

"What happened?" Eloise came rushing over wearing her gardening gloves and hat. "What is that?" She pointed toward my ankle. "Where are your shoes?"

I looked down and noticed I was back in my old clothes and there was blood dripping from what looked like a claw scratch.

"June," Eloise eyes turned dark. "Where have you been?"

I shook my head and held my ankle in pain.

"I've only ever seen this one other time." Eloise picked a stem off the aloe plant. "It was when another villager got a hex put on them."

Madame Torres glowed from my bag. I raked it toward me and pulled her out.

"You have got some really bad ju-ju following you around." The plump girl eyed me up and down. "Which means someone has put a bad hex on you."

Madame Torres reminded me of what the girl told me at Hidden Hall.

"When did you go to Hidden Hall?" Eloise dabbed the aloe on my scrape. "Have you encountered any unknown Dark-Sider along the way?"

As if my intuition light flipped on, Adeline popped into my head.

Was Adeline a spiritualist? A Dark-Sider? An evil Dark-Sider?

Chapter Twenty-one

The more I thought about my relationship with Adeline, the more I believed my intuition was telling me something.

It could be true. She might be a spiritualist. I had no clue I was a spiritualist until I moved to Locust Grove.

"Do you think you are going to be okay?" Eloise asked.

After she had doctored up whatever evil spirit had tried to do to me, I rested on the couch with a nice cup of tea left over from the ruined tea meeting with the Marys.

"I'll be fine." I worried about Eloise. I knew she was hurting about Oscar. He would never know he had an Aunt in Whispering Falls since he denounced his gift. "Are you?"

"You know." She picked at her short red hair. Her emerald eyes filled with tears. "I lived without him for over twenty years. As long as I see him through you, I'm going to be okay." She clasped her hands and changed the subject. "Any breakthroughs? Have you heard from Mac?"

"No." I fluffed up the pillow behind me and leaned back. "But while I was at the funeral home, Faith and Petunia were having a field day accusing me of all of the crimes."

"Why would they do that? They are your friends." Eloise slipped into the kitchen before returning with the steaming teapot to refill my cup.

"Some friends they are." I blew on the hot liquid before I took a sip. I did need to talk to Mac. I wasn't getting any closer to solving the crime. I guess I was going to have to tell him what I knew and about their threatening me.

"Did you tell Oscar?" She had a faraway look in her eyes.

"No, but that's a good idea." I bit my lip. "So, do you think I could slip out of here without the Marys finding out?"

"*The Marys.*" Her jaw clenched. "I'll take care of the Marys. You have to do what you have to do."

"You can take care of the Marys?" I laughed. "They can't take care of themselves."

After gathering a few things, like Belur and Madame Torres, I made a trek through the woods to get the Green Machine.

Keep me safe. I felt my wrist for my charm bracelet. I hadn't seen Mr. Prince Charming since the funeral and I needed all the protection I could get. Wrinkling my brow, I had forgotten that I hadn't gotten my bracelet back from Bella. She was going to give it to me the night of the ceremony, but then, Kenny happened.

"Fine," I pictured my bracelet sitting on the counter in Bella's Baubles and thrust my fist to the side. "Nice."

I smiled, standing in the middle of the shop. No one was there, but a sound from the back told me I wouldn't be alone for long. Reaching out, I picked up my bracelet exactly where I had envisioned it. I turned to face the windows and looked across the street at Wicked Good.

Faith was putting an armload of Wicked Good boxes in the cupcake car before she jumped in and zoomed off.

The sound of footsteps made me rush to think about the front seat of the Green Machine. In no time, I was in the driver's seat with the car in neutral as it rolled down the hill before I turned over the engine to make my way out of town.

The bracelet jingled even more with the purple pendent dangling a little lower than the rest of the charms as I gripped and re-gripped the steering wheel.

Oscar's cop car was in his driveway so I pulled in. If what Faith said about Officer Gandolf telling people he was here to assist in the investigations, and he didn't tell them Oscar was put in sorcerer school, then Oscar could slip into Whispering Falls and ask a few questions.

"Hey," I jumped out of the car just as Oscar was locking up the side door. "You going somewhere?"

"Yeah, work." He turned the key. His strong jaw muscles flicked with each chew of his gum. He looked at me with a blank stare. Not the same twinkle in his eye a few days ago when he kissed me good morning.

Tormented by confusing emotions, I swallowed hard. "Do you have a minute? It's about the case."

He lifted up the cuff of his shirt and peered at his watch. He held up his hand. "Five minutes." He unlocked the door and I followed him inside.

"It will only take a minute." I paced back and forth in his kitchen and quickly explained the situations with Faith and Petunia. "Both of them will act like they know you, and *really* well, since I talk about us all the time."

"Us? All the time?" His mouth spread into a thin-lipped smile.

"You know," I wiggled my finger between the two of us. "We go together like peas and carrots." If he only knew how well I did know him…but I had to shake off those thoughts. For now, those days were over. "Anyway, just pretend like you know them as well as they know you. Stick with the questions by doing the cop thing that you do. Don't let them question you, because they are out to get me."

"First of all, I don't know what you said to the…" He looked at his notebook where he had been taking notes on what I was saying. "Short hair, blonde…Faith. But you can't go around telling people how to run their business. You have never been in the newspaper business."

"Right." I nodded. If he only understood it wasn't just a newspaper business. I listened patiently.

"And Petunia's appearance scares me a little." He tapped the notebook with the pen. "She has an ostrich that you are accused of stealing the feathers from/ Now you are some sort of city council president and she wanted the job?"

His questions were between the spiritual and physical world and were making me confused.

"All I'm asking is that you ask them questions about Kenny, if they knew him and where they were during all the other crimes." I waved my hand around trying to avoid the hot hunk staring at me in amusement. It was difficult not to grab him, shake him, and tell him we are a couple. A real true romance, kissing and all. But I knew that wouldn't help matters. What was done was done.

That won't stop me from trying to spark some memory. Only that would have to happen after this whole mess was cleared up.

"Fine." He gestured toward the door. "I've got to get going. Shouldn't you be working?"

"They are investigating the shop," I muttered. "When do you think you can go?"

"Tonight, maybe."

I squealed and threw my arms around his neck. In a momentary lapse of what had happened, I grabbed the sides of his face and kissed him so hard I thought I was going to pass out.

"Umm. . ." He pulled away. Confusion set in his deep, dark eyes. His face was beet red. "That was weird."

"Oh," I put my hands up to my lips. "I'm so sorry. I just believe that if I have any chance of getting out of this, you can help me."

"Okay." He rushed to his car as if he was running from the plague. "I'll call you."

I stood in his driveway as he skidded out of it so fast, the gravel spit from underneath his tires.

"Great." I mumbled before another car came barreling down the street, and not just any car, a car with a big cupcake on top.

Chapter Twenty-Two

"Okay," I kept a good distance between the Green Machine and the cupcake, "Where are you going?"

Every turn Faith made, I made. Every swerve she made, I did the same, until she pulled into the Piggly Wiggly.

Dang! She was there delivering some baked goods. I watched as she got out of the cupcake car and grabbed a few of the packages before she disappeared into the store.

"Now what am I going to do?" I surveyed the lot to see if I saw Adeline's car. I had only seen it a couple of times parked in front of A Charming Cure, so it was possible that I really didn't know what it actually looked like. I beat my fingers on the wheel as I looked around.

It would be a great time to question her about the June's Gems or even her thoughts about me not giving her a potion.

Glancing back to the cupcake car, a thought snapped into my head. What if none of the crimes are related to each other, but are only related because of me? Did Petunia kill Kenny because she was so out of her mind when they named me the village president that she couldn't think straight? Or did the Karima sisters kill him because I was trying to save the world and they needed a dead body? What if Faith broke into Wicked Good to take the June's Gems, making it seem like I did it? Then there was the ostrich…Petunia, Faith *and* the Karimas knew I was trying to help catch the bird. Never mind the reason behind it, but I know each of them had their grubby little paws in it.

Then there was Adeline. Love was a wonderful motive to kill. I couldn't help but think if I didn't give her what she wanted, then she was seeking revenge.

Out of the corner of my eye, Faith came high stepping out and got in the cupcake car.

Where are you going? I watched her as she pulled the car to the side of the building and not out of the parking lot. She got out of the car and leaned up against it. Her long blonde hair glistened in the sun and her tan legs looked a mile long. *George*?

Adeline's hot hunky George propped himself up with one arm, while his other hand flicked Faith's hair behind her shoulder.

No. Shock and awe set in. Was George cheating on Adeline? Yes!

I rapidly blinked my eyes. Did Raven know about this? No wonder Adeline had always come to the shop to get potions to make sure George was in love with her.

"That nogoodsonofa…" I gritted my teeth, remembering how much George loved the June's Gems. "Poor Faith."

Even though I wasn't sure why Faith would frame me or be so angry when all I was trying to do was help her get better at her predictions, I still cared for her and didn't want her to get used for the chocolatey treat.

My skin crawled watching George play up his good looks and Faith soaking it in.

"I wish I could see Raven and tell her about this." I put the car in drive and headed out of the parking lot.

Reaching into my bag, I pulled Belur out. He was glowing. I put him on the seat next to me and then retrieved Adeline's address that was wadded up in the bottom.

I popped off the lid of Belur's jar.

"Do you want something?"

Two little puffs of smoke came out of the bottle like the little engine that could before Belur appeared in the passenger seat.

"I just don't understand why you won't let me come out." His bottom lip was plump as he pouted. "I get tired of staying in that little bottle all day long."

He cracked and popped as he put his hands way above his head and stretched them to the sky.

"Because, I don't want a genie." I ignored Madame Torres glowing in my bag. "I can barely handle the crystal ball I own, much less a genie."

"But you are my master." He crossed his arms. "I do not feel worthy."

"You are worthy, just not for me." I tapped the top of his bottle and in a flash he was gone. I tucked him back in the bag where he would be safe and sound until I figured out what to do with him. But, first things first.

Adeline.

The street she lived on was tree-lined on both sides, creating a beautiful canopy over the road as I made my way toward her house.

Just like every other house in Locust Grove, she owned a small Cape Cod that was much older than she was. Her car was nestled in the driveway.

Did she come straight here from Kenny's funeral? Did she know that George was cheating on her?

The first time she came in the shop, she had a sneaky suspicion he was cheating on her, and that was when I gave her the June's Gems. She said she'd do anything to keep him. Does that mean she would steal June's Gems from the Wicked Good?

Even though she was getting them delivered to the Piggly Wiggly now, a few days ago she wasn't receiving June's Gems. I wanted to know exactly why she was at Kenny's funeral.

The window shades were drawn. Tapping on the door, I looked around. The flowerbed running along the front of the house was neatly kept and the yard was perfectly manicured.

"June?" Adeline's short hair was sticking up all over the place. Her eyes were half closed. She didn't look like she had only a couple of hours ago. "What are you doing here?"

"I told you that I was going to come over to do some yoga." I lied. She stood like a brick fireplace, not moving. I had to worm my way in there somehow. "And I had a feeling you weren't up to your best."

"You're right." She didn't look amused. "I thought I told you to call me."

"You did, but I went by the Piggly Wiggly and you weren't there, so I thought I'd take a chance." I shrugged.

"You went to the Piggly Wiggly?" She held the door open. I couldn't help but think I was walking into a lion's den. "Did you see George?"

"I didn't see your car, so I didn't go in." I was vague in my answer. "So what is going on with you?" There was no way I was going to get anything out of her by beating around the bush.

"Come on in." I followed her into a magical place of its own.

The gray colored foyer was neat and decorated with black hardwood floors and there was wainscoting on the bottom half the wall. A delicate crystal chandelier hung from the center of the ceiling.

I followed her into her kitchen that was just as charming as the foyer. The whitewashed kitchen cabinets and stainless steel farm sink went perfectly with her butcher block island and lacey window treatments.

"I love your house." Everything was nice and neat and in its place. A sure sign of a perfectionist killer, I noted.

"Thanks. I'm a shabby chic kinda girl." She smirked. She held up the freshly made pot of coffee. "I'm a little tired. I've been burning at both ends lately. Do you want a cup?"

"No, I'm fine."

I bet you have been burning at both ends. I wanted to point a finger at her and ask her point blank why she was at Kenny's funeral, if she killed him, and if she broke into Wicked Good, but I had to proceed with caution.

"Do you want to tell me what is going on?"

"No." She shook her head as she slowly poured cream and sugar in her coffee. "I'm taking care of it."

"You don't want me to get you a remedy?"

She stiffened, her jaw clenched, and she stopped stirring. "You couldn't help me a few days ago. Why are you so eager to help now, June?"

"I…" I didn't like the way she asked. "I need to use your bathroom real quick."

"Fine." She pointed in the opposite direction from which we came from. "Second door on the right."

I couldn't get to that second door quick enough. From behind the door, I took a big whiff. Something had to come to me. I had to tap into Adeline's soul and see if she was going to kill me.

"What have I gotten myself into?" I murmured.

"What did you say?" Adeline asked. There was a small shadow coming from the crack at the bottom of the door.

"I love your bathroom too." I lied again, and bent down to put my nose next to the crack, inhaling deeply.

She knows. The smell of a cheater filled my lungs. She was a woman scorned and she was going to do what she needed to do to keep George.

Did she plan on breaking into A Charming Cure to steal a potion the night Kenny died and Kenny got in her way? When that backfired, did she resort to breaking into Wicked Good?

Was George next?

Oh no! Faith's beautiful little face came to mind. Was Faith next?

Thrusting my fists to the side, I knew I had to do something before it was too late.

Chapter Twenty-Two

"I'm loving this," I whispered when I landed in A Charming Cure, referring to the teletransporting gift. The shop was dark and dusty, it had only been a couple days since any customers had walked through the door. The place looked dead.

The drapes were pulled, a few of my precious bottle looked like they had been taken, probably from Officer Gandolf, and it was freezing.

Luckily, I knew the place like the back of my hand so I didn't have to turn on the light to feel my way around. All I had to do was count down the ingredients on the shelf to know exactly what I needed for the first potion.

There were two cures I needed to put together before I came out of Adeline's bathroom. I had to work fast. I could only pretend to be going to the bathroom for so long before she got suspicious.

I had to get Oscar to Adeline's house without telling him why. I had to get him a lead. I hated to put magic into it, but I had to protect George and Faith from turning up dead like Kenny. And I couldn't directly go to anyone because I didn't have any proof.

What was I supposed to do? Go to Oscar and tell him I had a hunch? I couldn't tell him that I'm a spiritualist – well, it would be a witch in his vocabulary.

Flipping the cauldron on, I went down the row.

1, 2, 3, 4. I counted the ingredients.

"Wormwood." I took the bottle from the shelf knowing it was a great ingredient to help banish anger. Anger was one thing that needed to immediately be taken from Adeline. Going back down the line, I gathered the bottle of graveyard dirt for a little sleepy time and a couple sprigs of spearmint to help Adeline breathe in some clear thoughts.

With Adeline in mind, I threw in the ingredients in no particular order. There wasn't time to go slow. I had to get this potion to her. I needed her to go to sleep so I could get to Oscar.

The bubbling oily tonic, that is black with crimson, glows. It smells exactly like vegetable soup, but with a hint of chocolate.

That was the strange part about being a homeopathic spiritualist. When I make a potion with a specific person in mind, the potion takes on the smells and tastes of the recipient. The vegetables didn't smell good to me, but the chocolate smelled delicious!

With the substance at a fast boil, I put my hands over the cauldron and chanted, "Angels of power, Angels of might, Let Adeline sleep through a few days and nights."

The cauldron shut off and the liquid stopped rolling. A bright denim glowed from the empty bottle shelf, illuminating the dark shop. The bottle let me know it was the one that I had to put the potion in and somehow get it down Adeline's throat.

Just looking at and holding the flask with the enamel light pink roses and light green stems made me relaxed. It was perfect for a few days sleep.

Setting it aside, I had to get to work on a potion for Oscar. Thank goodness he wasn't a spiritualist anymore or I wouldn't be able to do this. I had to get him to Adeline's house. This potion was guaranteed to not only get him there, but to put the suspicion in his mind to investigate her for the crimes. He won't stop until he figures it out. He might not know he's in love with me and I'm the one for him, but he does know he can't stop helping me until he figures it out.

Quickly, I cleaned out the cauldron so the potions didn't mix. The last thing I needed was the only person on my side sleeping on the job as well as the suspect sleeping. That wouldn't solve anything.

"Dirt." I bit my lip. I needed dirt from the Locust Grove police station. This potion is meant to be sprinkled around Adeline's house to attract the police. "Dang."

I thrust my fist to the side with the front of Locust Grove's Police Department in mind and instantly I was standing there. I hurried to the side in fear someone might see me. The last thing I needed was to explain to Oscar, if I saw him, where my car was.

"Hey, man." A male voice boomed from the front of the building. "Where are you off to?"

"I have to run into Whispering Falls for a few minutes." Oscar answered the man's question.

I peeped around the brick building and saw Oscar standing on the sidewalk with another officer.

"I'm doing June a favor." He shuffled his feet.

"When are you going to tell her?" The man asked.

Tell me? Tell me what? I leaned in a little more.

"It has all changed since she moved to Whispering Falls." He squinted in the sunlight as he looked up. "It's like she is too busy to remember our friendship, much less have time to go on a date."

"If you don't do it now, you might lose her."

Oscar shrugged. "She's been acting a little strange lately. All this talk of voodoo and crap. I think I've already lost her to that silly little town."

"Cut your loss and find a new girl." They guy slapped him on the back with an evil grin. "I've got a girl that will show you a good time anytime you want, if you know what I mean."

Oscar shook his head. "I'll keep that in mind."

Oh! No! You! Won't. I glared at the other guy. "I wish you would just disappear," I whispered.

Right in front of my eyes, the officer was gone.

"Don?" Oscar turned in circles looking for his friend.

Did I just do that? Shock and awe took over my soul. I really had to read the Powers of the Village President manual that Izzy had left for me. But I had been a little busy trying to stay out of jail and being the president to do any reading.

"I wish you would reappear." Reluctantly, I pictured the officer and just as the last word left my mouth, he stood next to Oscar again.

"Dude, how did you do that?" Oscar asked with a confused look on his face.

"What?" Don's eyebrows came together in a scowl. "Man, that girl has got you seeing things."

Oscar rubbed his eyes. "Yea, I guess." He shook his head like he was trying to shake out his mind what he had just seen. "I've gotta get out of here."

"Give me the word and I've got you a date!" The officer yelled after Oscar.

Without turning around, Oscar waved his hand in the air. I gathered a little dirt and glared at the officer before I disappeared back to the shop.

Mewl, mewl. Mr. Prince Charming sat next to the cauldron.

"It's about time you showed up." I threw the dirt in the cauldron and dusted my hands off. "Some fairy-god cat you are. I had to go steal my bracelet and solve my own crime. Which by the way, I do believe Adeline is knee deep in."

I really wanted to believe she was the mastermind behind the crimes, but I couldn't rule out Petunia and Faith.

"I just wish Raven was able to talk to me." I knew if I could talk to her about what I saw, she might be able to clear up some of my muddy intuition feelings.

Meow, meow. Mr. Prince Charming stretched out his paws and yawned before he curled up on the counter.

"Why do I get all the mismatched spiritual tools: A lazy fairy-god cat, a cranky crystal ball, and a big purple blob?" I tapped down the ingredient shelf to start working on my potion for the perimeter of Adeline's house. Only one problem, the potion called for the mixture to be dripped off the plucked feather of a macaw.

So that meant I had to make a pit stop at Glorybee.

"A dash of laurel, a pinch of mint and a skosh of sage should do the trick." I flipped on the cauldron once the fixings were in.

The moving, chunky substance was amber in color with blue oddiments. Taking a whiff, it smelled exactly like

Oscar's natural scent of pine and wood, but I knew it was going to taste just like Chinese---one of his favorites.

"Higady, digady, flong. Bring Oscar to Adeline's and feel something is wrong." I waved my hands over the liquid right before it shut off. The onyx bottle glowed yellow from the far left of the bottle shelf. Grabbing it, I quickly used the small ladle to drip the potion into it.

There wasn't much more time to waste. I had to get over to Glorybee, get a feather from that macaw and get back to Adeline's bathroom. I glanced at the clock, it seemed like I'd been gone for an hour, but in real time, it had only been ten minutes.

Gathering all my potions and putting them in my bag, I pictured Mr. Prince Charming and me underneath the tree in Glorybee without anyone else around before I thrust my fists to the side.

Squawk, squawk! The macaw flapped and flopped as Mr. Prince Charming made his way to the top of the tree.

"Yes, be sure to get a big fat feather." I ordered Mr. Prince Charming. "A big one so we don't screw this potion up."

I wasn't going to risk just any feather from that macaw.

"Hey there, hey there." The macaw held a leg up toward a creeping Mr. Prince Charming. "Bad ostrich, bad ostrich."

Mr. Prince Charming stopped, watching the bird dance from one clawed foot to the other.

"I really like your wings," he chirped. "Yes, I like them."

"I do like your wings, but I only need one feather." I begged the macaw.

"Got the wrong bird, wrong bird." He spread his wings out and the feathers on his back fanned around him before he jumped from the limb.

Hiss, hiss. Mr. Prince Charming batted at the air as the bird soared over top of me. I reached up and grabbed a fistful. Feathers flew all over the place.

"Wrong bird, wrong bird!" The macaw squealed.

"What is going on here?" The lights of Glorybee turned on as I thrust my fist to the side.

"Are you okay in there?"

I was back in Adeline's bathroom and a little shaken. Am I ever going to get use to these new powers? My stomach was a little queasy when I realized I had left Mr. Prince Charming to face the music.

"I'm fine," sniff, sniff, "I just got back from a funeral for a friend of mine in Whispering Falls and I thought that I was going to be okay."

Dead silence.

"And that's why I came." I paused to see if I could hear anything from the other side of the door. I reached over and flushed the toilet as if I had used it before I opened the door. "I thought some yoga could help me."

Adeline's eyes were as big as the full moon. Did I throw her off guard? Was her mind reeling, wondering if I saw her return to the city of the crimes?

"I'm so sorry." She followed closely behind me. "I had no idea."

I busted out crying like I was torn up. I actually *was* torn up thinking she was trying to get away with pinning these crimes on me.

"Was it the Indian?" She disappeared into the other room, leaving me alone with her cup of tea.

I pulled the rose potion bottle out of my bag and tapped a few drops in her tea before she returned with a couple of tissues.

"It was." I blew my nose. "They still don't know who killed him. Which reminds me," I wiped my eyes with the other tissue to really play the role, "why were you at A Charming Cure that night?"

"I…" She paced back and forth, wringing her hands together. The phone rang. "I'll be right back."

Dang! It looked like she was going to tell me something.

"June, I have to go." She slipped her feet into a pair of beige flip-flops, while taking a big ole drink of her tea. She grabbed her keys off the counter. "There is a mess with the deliveries at the Piggly Wiggly and I have to go straighten it out."

She showed me to the door. I sat in my car until her car was out of view. Jumping out, I grabbed the feather and the other potion from deep within my bag. Slowly, I walked around her house, dousing the feather with the potion and flinging it on the foundation as I chanted, in a low voice,

"Higady, digady, flong. Bring Oscar to Adeline's and feel something is wrong."

"Who are you?"

I jumped nearly out of my skin when a voice came from behind me.

"I'm a friend of Adeline's." *Right now would probably be a good time to get out of here.* My brain wasn't working. How could it? The man standing with his hand resting on a concealed gun didn't mind letting me know that he didn't care if I saw it or not. It was the man I saw in Adeline's office through the crystal ball.

"You are?" He questioned me, but there was a sneaky suspicion in his voice that in no way did he believe me.

"Yes, I am." I couldn't decide whether to go to the right or left of him to make my escape.

If I went to the right, I could jump in the neighbor's bushes if he started to shoot. I didn't know which would hurt worse, the rose bush thorns or his bullets.

If I went left, I'd just smack into Adeline's brick house. Which didn't sound pleasant either.

"You can see she isn't here, so you best be getting on your way." He shooed me away with his hand.

Without waiting for another wave of his hand, I darted to the right. I didn't look back to see if he had drawn his gun or even watched me go.

The wheels squealed when I put the pedal to the metal in the Green Machine.

Chapter Twenty-Three

"You won't believe what I uncovered today." There was no way I was going to tell Eloise about the gunman. She'd never let me out of her sight then. "I went to Kenny's funeral, and. . ."

"You what?" Eloise put the metal container on the counter. Her eyebrows dipped as she frowned. She had to have spent most of the day cleaning out her incense burners. They were lined up along the counter and on the island. This was a clear sign she had talked with Izzy about doing a full Whispering Falls cleanse, but I didn't ask her. The less I knew about what was going on outside of my own trauma, the better.

"I had to." I tapped my stomach. "Something told me I needed to go, and I'm glad I did."

"Did anyone see you?"

"No, I used my new powers to turn into a fairy." I smiled.

"A Fairy?"

"A pink Fairy." I nodded. "And I was a pretty good Fairy."

"What power are you talking about?"

I looked up and caught a concerned look on her face.

"The new powers with being the village president." I reminded her of what Izzy had said during the smudging ceremony before my life was twisted up like a ball of yarn.

"I'm not sure I know what you are talking about." She looked me over with a critical eye. "Maybe I don't know what I'm talking about."

No kidding. I brushed the notion that she didn't know about the powers when she was standing right there. She did have a lot on her mind. Not to mention the loss of Oscar.

"Anyway, go on." She picked up the long chain she used to swing her burner and took a towel to shine it.

"No one recognized me and it's the same ole, same ole with the people here." I sat down on the stool and planted my elbows on the kitchen island so I could rest my head.

I was actually a little tired from all of the running around and teletransporting I had been doing.

"Adeline, the customer that is always asking me about love potions," I reminded her, "was there. Why would she be there?"

Eloise raised an eyebrow. I had her complete attention. "Go on."

"Not only that, but I went to Locust Grove to ask her some questions. I started at the Piggly Wiggly, but she wasn't there." I leaned in a little. "Faith was though."

"Faith Mortimer?"

"Yes!" I smacked my hand on the island top. "It's not strange that she would be there delivering some bakery good for the Piggly Wiggly to sell, since Adeline also loves June's Gems."

Eloise backed up, using the counter for support. Her mouth was gaped open. "So Adeline ordered some June's Gems?"

"Yes, but that's not all." I continued to tell her about Faith and her little tryst with George, Adeline's boyfriend, who she bought the June's Gems for to keep him from breaking up with her.

"She had to have killed Kenny and broke into Wicked Good." Eloise rubbed her chin. "But why did she kill Kenny?"

"I'm not sure if she or her shaggy-haired hitman killed Kenny." I played with my charm bracelet, wondering where Mr. Prince Charming was, and if he got out of Glorybee without Petunia seeing him.

"June." A heavy sigh left her lips. "I draw the line at a hitman."

"Regardless, I think she knows George is cheating on her with Faith." I bit on the inside of my cheek. Dang, I wish I had a Ding Dong. "So I gave her a sleepy potion that will cloud her mind and not kill anyone until I get something figured out, or until Oscar can get some information."

"Oscar?" Her face lit up like the stars in the sky on a clear, Whispering Falls night. "You saw Oscar?"

"I did, and he doesn't remember anything about being sheriff of Whispering Falls." I hated to tell her that because it meant that he didn't remember her.

"Oh." Eloise looked down and picked at the edge of her fingernail. "What did he say about the case?"

"I asked him to come here and ask Raven, Faith, and Petunia a few questions."

"He can't come here!" Eloise's deep green cloak swished as she paced back and forth. "They don't know he was stripped of his powers."

"I know." I assured her. "I told him they were going to pretend like they knew him really well because I talk about him all the time."

Without a word, disappointment was displayed all over her face.

"So I guess I shouldn't tell you I put a spell around Adeline's house that will attract Oscar."

"No you shouldn't have." She grabbed a couple of herbs before she stuck them in a metal incense container and lit them on fire. She started to chant. The smoke billowed out as she swung the long chain back and forth.

She looked like she had gone off into a faraway place. There was no sense in trying to talk to her, so I slipped out when I noticed there was a glow coming from my bag.

I headed out of the house and down the gravel path. I needed privacy to see who needed what. I couldn't tell by the glow if it was Belur or Madame Torres.

"You are skating on thin ice." Mac McGurtle stood up. His black suit was a little more wrinkled than usual.

Mac McGurtle and Mary Ellen, one of the Marys, were having a cup of tea in the gazebo.

So much for privacy. I held my bag close to my body to help shield the glow. I didn't care if they saw Madame Torres, but I needed to keep Belur under-wraps. Having to explain him would look like I killed Kenny to keep the genie.

"Mary Ellen was good enough to inform me that you are leaving the premises." He looked over at Mary Ellen, who wouldn't even look at me.

Traitor. I eyed her and her fancy black one-piece jump suit and bright yellow heels. When the sun hit directly on her jeweled necklace, I had to look away or my eyes would probably have been burned.

"It's for your own good and the future of this community." She played with her long black ponytail that she had pulled so tight it looked like she had gotten a Botox job.

"We are lucky she didn't tell the other Marys or you would be banned." Mac walked over and rested his hands on the front of his suit coat. "You have to let Gandolf finish processing the evidence before we can start doing a lot of our own investigation."

They both looked at me like I should be saying something back, but I didn't. I didn't have time to process all he was saying, because Mr. Prince Charming was dancing around the herb garden. His tail was pointing in the direction of the Gathering Rock.

I held my bag tighter. There was a warm spot coming from it where the glow was getting brighter.

"Fine," I shouted as I darted out of the garden.

"June?" Mac's voice echoed throughout the garden. "Where are you going? You'd better not leave this forest!"

Yea, yea. Taking idle threats wasn't my strong suit. I kept my eye on a dancing Mr. Prince Charming. He ran like the wind through the forest and stopped just shy of the Gathering Rock.

Raven was sitting on the rock, staring into the woods.

"Good boy!" She clapped her hands together when Mr. Prince Charming darted to her side.

"Raven?" I kept my toes on the border of the woods and the edge of the community city limits.

"Thank you for coming." She stood up and walked over. "I know you can't cross the line, but I need your help. Faith needs your help."

"Tell me."

"I know you didn't break into Wicked Good, but I can't be so sure Faith didn't do it and pin it on you." She wrung hands together. "Ever since she started doing all the deliveries to other communities, she's been acting strange."

I let her talk, and watched as she nervously paced back and forth.

"She has never been out of a spiritual community. We went straight from our family home, to Hidden Hall, A Spiritualist University, to here." She shook her head. "I should've warned her about the dangers of the outside world, the temptations."

"What temptations?" I couldn't tell her I saw Faith and she might be in grave danger if Adeline knows about the affair.

"I think she met a guy, because she is doing all sorts of strange deliveries at night." She looked up, tears flooding down her cheeks. "I don't care if she dates a mortal; what I care about is that she hasn't made it to any of the other stops."

Oh, no! Did the potion I made for Adeline not work and did she make it to the Piggly Wiggly and catch George in Faith's arms?

"Don't worry." I wanted to grab her, but I was sure that the Marys might have an eye on me. "I'll help."

She nodded before she ran back down the hill toward Whispering Falls.

I did want to help. But how was I going to get out from under the Marys' prying eyes?

From the edge of the woods, there was a good view of my cottage and the Green Machine.

Mewl, mewl. Mr. Prince Charming did his figure eights around my ankles, letting me know I had to do what I had to do and he was going to protect me.

"You're right." I looked down. The glow from my bag reminded me that I had to see who needed me. Opening the bag, Madame Torres was bright-eyed and bushy-tailed with a not-so-nice grin on her face. I pulled her out.

"It's about time." She glared; her purple eye shadow matched her cheeks, but not her bright red lips. "You want me to inform you about things, but you ignore me. Which is it, June?"

"I don't have time to argue with you." I held her up, a stern look on my face. "What is going on?"

The inside of the ball swirled and twirled like a hurricane. There was anger brewing deep within the ball. The waves crashed up against the glass. I held her at arm's length in fear the ball was going to burst, the maddening water was thrashing so hard against the glass.

Suddenly the waters calmed and the waves parted.

"Faith?" I pulled Madame Torres closer. Faith was bound and gagged. Her beautiful blonde hair looked dull and her electric onyx eyes were dark and scared. I squinted to see if I could see anything else in the globe. A clue to where she was.

A pair of feet in beige flip-flops stood next to her, but I couldn't see the rest of the person. The tile reminded me of Adeline's office at the Piggly Wiggly.

Beige flip-flops?

Hiss, hiss. Mr. Prince Charming batted the air.

"Adeline has her!" I threw Madame Torres in the bag and thrust my hands to the side. I didn't care if the Mary's knew I was gone or not. I had to save Faith from a scorned Adeline.

Chapter Twenty-Four

I stood on the side of the Piggly Wiggly. I made sure I didn't teletransport inside in case someone saw me. The cupcake car was gone, but Adeline's was there. I hoped I wasn't too late.

The Piggly Wiggly was busy. Customers were in every aisle. I headed over to produce. Maybe George was there and I could use him for backup.

There he was, stacking the Gala apples in a perfect pyramid.

"Hi, George," I spoke quietly. "I'm not sure if you remember me. . ."

"Yea," He smiled. I could see how Faith and Adeline fell in love with his playboy looks. He was handsome and his smile was to die for. Not like Oscar, but pretty close. "You're June from that little shop."

"Yes." I looked around to make sure there weren't any customers present. "I'm looking for Adeline."

"I haven't seen her." He cut the lid of the last box of apples and started to stack those. "She said she wasn't feeling good and for me to take care of the all the deliveries."

"Did you call her about an hour or so ago telling her there was a delivery problem?" I questioned. I had to see if he knew what was going on.

Out of the corner of my eye, the hitman was coming through the front sliding doors.

"Okay, there is no time for this." I grabbed George by the arm and shielded myself from the hitman seeing me. He was obviously there because Adeline had called him about a tied-up Faith Mortimer.

What was he going to do? Off her here? Or take her tied-up and off her somewhere else?

"What are you doing?" George jerked away. "Maybe you need to take a few of your own herbs from that wacky shop that Adeline believes in so much."

Whacky shop? Okay, I'd let that one slide until after we saved Faith and Adeline was in the loony bin or jail where she deserved to be.

"Maybe so, but I think Adeline knows about your affair with Faith from the Wicked Good Bakery in

Whispering Falls." I rushed the words out of my mouth as his face dropped.

"You know about that?" There was an 'oh crap' cheater look on his face. There was panic in his voice. "Adeline knows?"

"Not only does she know, but I believe she has Faith tied up and about to have her hitman kill her and possibly you." My legs felt wobbly as I told him about Adeline's crazy rant. "I think she is responsible for the death of Kenny. . ." I knew he didn't know who Kenny was. "He was a supplier of mine for my *wacky shop*. You see, Adeline would do anything to keep you from never leaving her."

"You mean Kenny who is yea tall and Indian?" He held his hand over his head.

"Yea! You know him?" I turned George a little to the left as the hitman walked down another aisle. He was looking around and I could only assume he was looking for Adeline.

"He's the one who sold us the Ding Dongs." He talked fast. "As a matter of fact, Adeline was so mad when he told her they were discontinuing the line. She went crazy on him, right here in the store."

I gasped, panting in terror. She *did* kill Kenny. She *did* break into Wicked Good. She *did* plan to frame me for all the crimes, but it wasn't too late to save Faith.

If she did kill Faith, everyone would think that I did it. After all, Faith and I did have words and I skipped out of the forest like the Mary's told me not to.

"Kenny is dead," I whispered and turned him again when I saw the hitman go down a different aisle. " And I'm afraid Adeline is going to kill Faith."

"What?" George spat, shaking his head. "You are crazy."

"Just help me find Adeline in the store." I pointed out to the parking lot. "Her car is here. Go look if you don't believe me, and she has a hitman. I came face-to-face with him at her house this afternoon after I followed her from Kenny's funeral."

"She went to Kenny's funeral?" George was getting more and more confused the faster I talked.

"George!" I grabbed him, losing sight of the hitman. "I will explain all of this after we find Faith and Adeline. It's urgent."

"Fine." He grabbed my arm and tugged me along to the back of the store where Adeline's office was.

"Ouch," I shrugged. "That hurt."

"Well, you need to be pinched back into reality." He opened the office door and shoved me in.

"George, stop!" I screamed, not realizing he threw me into the midst of Adeline and Faith. Only Faith wasn't the only one tied up. So was Adeline.

Instantly my intuition took a blow to my gut.

My mouth dropped. I gasped, "George? You are the killer?"

Chapter Twenty-Five

"But, but." I stammered, looking dumbfounded between Faith, Adeline, and George, who had the box cutter held out in his hand.

"But, but, but." He mimicked me as he waved the knife in the air. "But nothing, you wack job. Did you really think you could use your mumbo jumbo to cure a love gone sour?"

I glanced over at Faith. She looked more scared than a ten-year-old kid seeing their first horror movie. Adeline glared at George. Her mouth was stuffed with panty hose that I was sure, or hoped George got out of the hygiene aisle.

The open and empty box of June's Gems from Wicked Good was on the desk.

"It seems like you enjoyed my namesake." I pointed toward the box.

"Shut up! If it weren't for Kenny coming in here and telling us that they weren't going to manufacture Ding Dongs, we wouldn't be in this mess." George pulled a spool of string from his back pocket. It looked like the string used to put asparagus stalks together. "But I knew there was an alternative, the June's Gems Adeline got from your stupid shop."

It was hard for me to concentrate on his words when he was dissing my shop and my spiritual gift. He eased closer with the thread taut between his outstretched hands.

"Wait." I put my hand up. "How did you know Kenny was going to be in Whispering Falls?"

"I knew he had your territory and I waited." His eyes narrowed as an evil grin crossed his lips. "He had to show up somewhere, sometime. So I confronted him about the Ding Dongs. I didn't spend all this time with little-miss-priss to be the veggie boy all my life. Ding Dongs were the money line of this place. It was because of him we were losing profits."

"Oh, Adeline. I'm so sorry." I put my hand on my gut. If only I would've listened to my intuition a little more, rather than thinking she was some crazy lovesick girl that would do anything to keep her man. I recalled seeing the symbol of money when she was at the shop, but completely dismissed it.

"But there was no apparent signs of struggle with Kenny." I remember Petunia mentioning something about a blow to Kenny's head was what killed him.

"There wasn't a struggle." George's eyes conveyed the fury within him. "When he turned his back on me, I shoved him as hard as I could, it was just like in the movies."

George acted out the way Kenny flung forward with his arms above his head. He even had the look of death on his face, just like I pictured Kenny had.

"It was great. He didn't see me coming, just like I didn't see how his little idea of stopping the snacks was going to affect my life." He snapped back into reality and pulled the string tight. "Now it's time to do something with you three!"

"What did Faith have to do with this?" I stalled for more time. I couldn't even wrap my head around the situation, and didn't know what to do.

"Sweet, sweet, innocent Faith." He licked his lips as if she was as tasty as a June's Gem. "She was going to be the substitute for Kenny. Since I was already in that crappy little town of yours, I decided to go in there and steal the recipe."

Faith looked down as he talked about her. A tear dripped off her chin and into her lap.

"Isn't that right, baby?" George's lips thinned as he hit her foot with his to get her to look at him, but she continued to look down. "Anyway, there wasn't a recipe in the whole damn shop, so I took every last June's Gem that was there."

George walked closer, putting the string closer and closer to my neck.

Damn! If I had long hair, he'd have to cut through that, instead of a direct shot with nothing in the way.

"What about Adeline?" I continued to ask questions as I tried to listen to my intuition.

"After I got the recipe for June's Gems, I was going to marry Adeline," he sighed, "only to lose her in a tragic accident on our honeymoon. But now I have this! I don't need her or you!"

He pulled papers that were folded in half out of his back pocket.

"Adeline was kind enough to think I wouldn't kill her if she went ahead and signed ownership of the Piggly Wiggly to me." His eyes clawed at me like talons. "But she was so wrong. All three of you are going to die."

Faith let out a little squeak, but Adeline had passed out. Her head hung to the side.

"What the hell?" George went over and pushed her arm with his foot. She fell over. "Shit. I didn't have to kill her. She did it herself." He cackled like the devil.

He was wrong. The potion had taken effect and she was out like a light. At least she wasn't going to have to watch our fate unfold.

"Now it's time to take care of you." George reached out. I thrust my hands and went straight into aisle five, landing on the hitman.

"You!" The shaggy man shoved me off. "You have been snooping around a little too much."

Instantly, my gut told me he knew the whole situation and feared he was working for George, not Adeline like I had originally thought.

"I…" I jumped to my feet with my bag still flung over my shoulder. Why on earth did I not teletransport to another place? I ran out of aisle five and across the produce section.

"You better stop right now if you know what is good for you!" The hitman's feet were thunderous behind me.

I stopped shy of the sliding front doors as George stood with his arms across his chest.

"Don't worry everyone." George swung the knife my way. "We have a shoplifter here. I'll just take her back to the office."

"Stop! Police! Drop the knife or I will shoot and it will hurt you worse than a little cut!" Oscar had his gun outstretched with one hand and a plastic salad container in the other.

George did exactly what he said.

"Kick it to me." Oscar ordered him. When George kicked it, Oscar put the salad down but kept the gun pointed at George. "June, pick up the knife."

I did what I was told, completely forgetting about the hitman. I handed the knife to Oscar.

"Put your hands up in the air and then place them behind your head." Oscar's voice echoed throughout the store. There was dead silence as George did what he was told.

Even at a time like this, Oscar was hot. Instantly my stomach felt better.

Faith? Adeline?

"Oscar, he has Faith and Adeline tied up in the office." I watched as Oscar put George in cuffs and then called for backup. "There is a hitman that works for him. He could be back there."

"June!" Faith screamed as she pushed past the hitman who was carrying Adeline. "You saved us!"

She threw her hands around my neck, and then around Oscars.

"Thank you so much, Oscar! You are a life saver!" She squeezed Oscar.

"I'm sorry, do I know you?" Oscar dazed at her.

"Oscar Park, are you okay?" Faith put her hand up to Oscar's forehead.

I stepped in-between them. Faith didn't know Oscar had denounced his spiritual gift and now was not the time to tell her.

"He is in his element. Shh," I whispered trying to get her to hush.

"Oh." Her eyes lifted. She leaned over with her hand next to her mouth. "This is exciting."

It *was* exciting to see Oscar in his element. And it was great to see Locust Grove's backup haul George off to the jail. I was pleased to hear the hitman was really a private investigator Adeline had hired to tail George.

All was well with the world...so far.

Chapter Twenty-Six

There was nothing better than the feeling of getting back to work…well, having Oscar back would top it, but I knew that wasn't going to happen. Once you denounce your spiritual side, it's gone forever.

At least that was all the research I had found when I got my Village President role back after the Order of Elders, otherwise known as the Marys, gave the okay after reviewing all the evidence proving I didn't kill Kenny.

I was lucky that Oscar was at the Piggly Wiggly that afternoon getting a salad for dinner. And I was relieved to realize Adeline had worked with Kenny for years, as did her father before her. She said she recognized him on the steps of my shop that night and felt like she needed to come to his funeral, and she recognized Faith at the funeral.

Adeline said Faith was hanging around the produce section a little too much and she hired the private investigator to keep an eye on her. He was the one who called the day I was at her house to tell her he had pictures of Faith and George kissing outside the Piggly Wiggly by the cupcake car.

She darted out the door, but the P.I. had told her to stay put because he knew she was upset. That's when he came to her house and found me putting the spell around her house.

Meow, meow. Mr. Prince Charming sat on the counter of A Charming Cure and batted at my charm bracelet as it dangled in the air as I brushed the potion bottles with the duster.

"Yes, I'm glad it's over." I put the duster down and walked over to the windows to pull the shades open.

The direct sunlight darted in the front windows. The shop came to life. All the bottles sparkled and gleamed. I couldn't help but look over at Glorybee. That was the only crime that hadn't been solved.

The ostrich was still missing, and we still didn't know where the animals had even come from. I hadn't seen Petunia since Kenny's murder had been solved, but I had a feeling she still believed I had something to do with that bird-napping.

Petunia was running around the shop, feeding all the animals. So I looked back at the clock. I saw Mr. Prince

Charming taking some time to clean himself. I had twenty minutes until the shops in Whispering Falls opened.

"I'll be right back," I told Mr. Prince Charming and set out for Glorybee.

I stopped just shy of the pet shop and turned around. Whispering Falls had never been so beautiful. All the cottage shop window boxes were in full bloom, bursting with every color of the rainbow. Each shop was in tip-top shape. Every storefront ornamental gate twinkled in the sunlight, giving off a magical feel that no one but the residents of Whispering Falls could explain.

"Here goes nothing." The overhead bell dinged when I walked in the door, letting Petunia know I was there.

"I wondered when you were coming to see me." She knew it was me before she turned around.

"I had to come over and see you." I had forgiven everything I overhead, when I was disguised as a fairy at the funeral. I knew she and Faith were hurt. "You have to know that I have nothing to do with the missing bird."

"Missing bird." *Squawk!* The macaw jumped around. "Really like your wings, like your wings."

"Why didn't anyone steal *him*?" Petunia threw a peanut up in the air and the macaw caught it. "Now I know how much Patience gets on Constance's nerves with her repeating."

Ugh. I doubled over with a shot to the gut. Words began to flood my head.

"I got the wrong bird. I really like your wings. Bad ostrich."

"Are you okay?" Petunia dropped the animal food on the floor and rushed over to me.

"Yes."

Patience.

"Petunia, I'll be back!" I grabbed the long stick with the noose at the end that Petunia was trying to rope the ostrich with and ran out the door and down the street toward Two Sisters and a Funeral.

If my hunch was right, and the way the macaw talked, my intuition told me Patience Karima's name was written all over this bird napping.

"Good boy, good boy!" Patience yelled. It was bouncing off all the walls in the funeral home.

I opened all the doors and stopped when I came to the last door.

"You are a bad ostrich!" She screeched right before I burst through the door.

The hardwood floor creaked under her ample girth as Patience swayed back and forth with her arms outstretched to the side. The ostrich stared her down, taking a jab here and there as she got closer.

Quickly I swung the pole over my head and wrapped the loop around the bird's neck.

"I...I..." Patience stuttered. "I can explain."

The ostrich darted out of the room with me holding on.

"Yes, you will!" I yelled with my feet in mid-air, holding on for dear life. "At your hearing in front of the Village Council tomorrow night!"

I tried to look back as the bird flung me all over Main Street on our way back to Glorybee. Patience stood on the steps of Two Sisters and A Funeral, sobbing into a handkerchief.

Izzy, Gerald, Bella, Faith, Raven, Constance, and Petunia stood on the street watching as I held on.

"Don't let go!" Petunia held the door open to Glorybee as the bird ran straight for her.

Once inside, I let go. The bird stopped at the bird feeders and started to peck, leaving a trail of a mess.

"How did you figure it out?" Petunia stroked the bird as if he had done something good.

"Let's say the macaw told me." I looked up at the macaw and winked.

"Good bird. Good bird." He danced from leg to leg on the top branch of the tree.

"You better get to work." Petunia continued to pet the ostrich while she nodded at the door.

A line had already formed in front of A Charming Cure.

Chapter Twenty-Seven

"That was crazy!" I pulled Madame Torres out of my bag at the end of the day.

There was one customer after another, which was good, because I didn't have time to think about Oscar and how I was going to win him back.

It was good to hear he had some feelings for me, at least that was what I thought I heard him say the day I was at the police station collecting dirt for a spell, but I couldn't be sure. I was in a fog then and my mind could have made up anything to believe Oscar was still in love with me.

"Yes it was." Madame Torres appeared a little more relaxed since the last time I saw her. "What are we going to do with *that*?"

I followed her eyes to Belur's bottle. There was a faint glow.

"I don't know." I popped the cork to let him out. He had been cooped up in there for quite a while now.

A stream of purple smoke danced out and into the air, filling the entire shop.

Cough, cough. I fanned the smoke.

"Don't you just love a grand entrance?" Belur's face had a smile that would light up the worst of days.

He was a pain in my butt, but he was very entertaining.

"I really wish I knew who you belong to." I smiled, shaking my head. It would have been nice to confirm he was Kenny's, but I guess I wasn't going to have any luck with that since Kenny was dead.

"Belur!" A very small Kenny look-a-like rushed through the front door of the shop. "I wondered where you were."

That was strange. The boy blew in with the wind. . .

"You…" I pointed at him after I recognized him. "You are Kenny's son."

"Yea, I'm KJ, Kenny Jr. How did you know?" He smiled, looking exactly like his father.

"I was at the funeral and saw you sitting on the side with your family." I couldn't tell him that I was dressed as a fairy.

"I'm sorry." He looked at me as if he was trying to recall seeing me. "There were so many people there."

"No, you don't have to apologize." I smiled back. "I'm sorry for your loss."

"Your wish is my command." Belur crossed his arms in front of him and stared at me. He didn't look KJ's way.

"Oh, no." KJ looked aggravated. He turned back to me. "You didn't make any wishes did you?"

"No!" Vigorously I shook my head.

"Did too!" Belur shouted as he floated in the air, glaring his big blue eyes at me.

"No, I didn't!" I shouted back.

"Um," Madame Torres appeared in her ball, "yes you did."

She disappeared, leaving the ball to play like a television screen of my thoughts and actions.

I wish I knew how to use a genie. I wish I could have a break in the murder. I wish I could teletransport like Aunt Helena. I wish I could be disguised so I could go to Kenny's funeral.

Madame Torres reappeared. "Do I need to play anymore of your wishes?"

My mouth dropped. "Do you mean I can't really teletransport?"

Madame Torres nodded. "Not without *that*." Her eyes darted toward Belur.

My memory flooded with all the cool stuff that I had been doing.

"So none of those cool powers are from being Village President?"

"Nope." Madame Torres was good at not sugar-coating anything.

Belur didn't say anything. He simply floated on his purple cloud with his lips tight.

"I'm sorry, but I'd like to have my genie back." KJ burst my bubble.

"Just one more wish?" I really wanted Oscar to remember us.

"No, I'm sorry." KJ picked up the bottle. "Belur!"

The air went dry as Belur was sucked back into the bottle. KJ stuck the lid on.

"The good news is that I'm going to be taking over for my dad." He smiled and pulled out a bundle of sage. "I think you need this."

He winked. . .and blew out with the breeze.

Chapter Twenty-Eight

It felt good getting to go back to the cottage and life as I had begun to know it.

"Are you ready to go to bed?" I rubbed down Mr. Prince Charming's back as he lay next to me on the couch.

After KJ left the shop, I was tired and didn't bother restocking the shelves. I made a plan to get up bright and early, maybe catch Eloise cleansing the streets of Whispering Falls, and grab a coffee at the Tea Shoppe before work.

That would give me plenty of time to stock the inventory before the shop opened.

Mewl, mewl. Mr. Prince Charming yawned, jumped off the couch and darted to the bedroom.

Knock, knock, knock.

"Who's here?" I glanced up at the clock. "It's ten o'clock."

I got up and pulled the shade on the door aside. Oscar was standing in the light of the moon.

"Hey!" I opened the door. I didn't care if I got any sleep tonight. The second we were together, time fell away from me.

"I thought I'd stop by and give you some of these." He held out a pink and green Wicked Good Bakery box. I didn't have to look to know what was in it.

"Come in." I held the door open. My legs went spongy. Seeing him made me miss him even more than I already had.

I had to look away from his lips. I felt like a breathless eighteen-year-old girl.

"Nah. I can't." His smile faded away. "I've got to get back to Locust Grove. I have to work early."

I took the box from him. Static electricity tingled between our fingertips.

"Oh." I pulled my hand away. "Thank you."

There was an odd distance between us, but a familiar look in his eyes.

"Are you sure you can't come in?" I asked again, hoping he'd change his mind.

"I can't." There was an odd twinge of disappointment on his face. My gut told me he wanted to, but time was going to have to be on our side.

Somehow, and sometime soon, I was going to have to let him in on my little secret of being a spiritualist.

"You need to come back when you can stay." I urged him.

"About that." He stood at the door with his hands in his jean pockets. "Do you want to grab a pizza tomorrow night?"

"Like a date?" Suddenly I was wide-awake.

"Something like that." He looked down at his feet and shuffled his foot on a loose piece of gravel.

"Great!" I didn't give him the opportunity to back out. "Be here by seven."

He looked up and smiled in approval before he started to walk away.

"You wouldn't believe what I discovered in this quaint little town you moved to." He rubbed his temples before he got in his car and zoomed off.

I had to go to bed and get my beauty sleep. After all, I was the new Village President who was going to have to figure out where these animals came from and why Patience had bird napped the ostrich. Not to mention, I needed to be on my game when I explain to Oscar that I'm not the girl who grew up next door to him.

I shut the door and leaned up against it, replaying the last words he spoke.

"You wouldn't believe what I discovered in this quaint little town you moved to."

"If only you knew," I whispered before I turned out the lights.

A Note From The Author

Thank you so much for reading my novel. I'm truly grateful for the time we have spent together. Reviews are very important to an author's career and I would appreciate it if you could take a couple minutes of your time by leaving a review for my novel. Thank you so much, and I hope we continue to meet in the world of books. ~Tonya Kappes

About The Author

International bestselling author Tonya Kappes spends her day lost in the world of her quirky characters that get into even quirkier situations.

When she isn't writing, she's busy being the princess, queen and jester of her domain which includes her BFF husband, her teenage guys, two dogs, and one lazy Kitty.

Tonya has an amazing STREET TEAM where she connects with her fans on a daily basis. If you are interested in becoming a Tonya Kappes Street Team member, be sure to message her on Facebook.

For more information, check out Tonya's website at Tonyakappes.com.

82117275R00159

Made in the USA
Columbia, SC
28 November 2017